The Tales of Bear Itaxsca
Crow Warrior and Bounty Hunter

By John David Young
With Teresa Whitehawk

Published by EagleBear Press
In conjunction with KDP and Create Space
Look for the Ebook on Amazon.com
Co-author and Editor – Teresa Whitehawk
All Authors rights reserved.
ISBN# 978-0-578-65984-8
Copyright 2020

INDEX OF STORIES

Title

Page

Bear Itaxsca
Crow Warrior and Bounty Hunter

By John David Young
with Teresa Whitehawk

I

    Bear Itaxsca was his name. A Crow Indian displaced by the War Between the States. He was tall, six feet two inches, and had just been released from service with the Union

Army. He served the War out as a scout and fighter, and now he was flung back into a world where he had no tribe, no money, no way of making a living except by bounty hunting.

The world was harsh for a Native, and only the Spanish hat, straight brimmed and black, shaded his dark eyes from the rising sun. He remembered the day he joined to fight the White Man's war. He was twenty and they came to the village seeking those who would join. Join the fight against slavery. He was impassioned because he had seen the slavers and their cruel getting of his Native brothers to die under a whip.

"I will fight for this!" he said to himself. He was thrust into a system, enslaved by it, taught the White Man's way of fighting and used it. He was taught to read, write, and figure. He was smart and tough. He killed all men that wore the grey, and a few more. Killing sickened his soul.

"It's over!" they shouted and he stood there, unthanked for his sacrifice. A uniform, a gun, and a good pair of boots. They said he could totter on back to his tribe or where ever, just as long as he got out of their hair.

Bear Itaxsca was alone with no one to respect him.

He traded a topaz ring for a fine pony, which was pure black, with white feet, and fire in his eye. Bear made his own saddle carved from a Yew tree, with the cured skin of an elk to cover it. He found a jacket made of Wolf skin with the hair of the beast still intact around the collar; the man it had belonged to was dead and he no longer needed it.

The one thing Bear Itaxsca did was stand tall. Guns he knew. He wore two Colt 36 caliber pistols and a .44 Navy Colt, stuck in the purple sash he wore around his waist, a Henry 45-

70 in his saddle sheath. His long knife, a fourteen-inch Bowie, was in its sheath strapped to his leg, hidden in the well-cared for Calvary boots, another gift from the army.

His eyes were expressionless, dark brown and ready for any advisory, at once predatory to all.

Bear needed to eat that day and he was well supplied. He'd killed a small deer and back strapped it so he had several chunks of venison in his pack. Just roasting it on a stick was not appealing to him; he would look for a cabin. In a couple of hours he came upon a small homestead and walked his horse down to the front gate.

"Hello the house," he said loudly. "Anyone at home?"

"What'd you want?" came a woman's reply from inside. "I got my rifle on you."

"No need, Ma'am." He answered. "I was just tired of camp cooking and I wondered if you'd like to share a backstrap of venison with me."

The door opened a crack. "You got deer meat?" the female voice asked.

"Yeah," he answered. "And I'll give it all to you if you do the fixin'."

"Oh God be blessed!" he heard her say. "Let me see it."

"It's in the bag," Bear answered. "I'll leave it on the porch."

He walked his horse to the edge of the porch and threw it down.

A woman, about thirty years old, poked her head out. "That'd be a life-saver, mister. My man's away, ain't had no good meat for days."

"If you cook it, it's all yours," Bear said.

"Tie up your horse." she said nervously. She snatched at the bag and Bear could hear the chatter of children behind her.

Bear sat there for a good ten minutes until she poked her head out the door again.

"Thank you, Mister." she said her voice a little on the shaky side. "I'll steak up some of this for you. Beans and potatoes?"

"Sounds good." Bear said. "I would like a table to sit at though."

"Go 'round back," she snapped. "There's a back porch there with a table and a chair."

Bear led his horse around the back and there was a rickety old table and an old carved chair. It used to be a rocker but someone had removed the rockers and put new legs on it. It would do. He relaxed, putting his Navy Colt on the table, cocked and loaded.

After some time, the woman came out with a steaming plate of food. Two big venison steaks sliced boiled potatoes and beans, all covered in gravy.

"Thank you, Mister," she said. "We were wondering what we were gonna do if my husband didn't get back from selling the cattle soon."

Bear looked at her closely. She was young, had a pleasing figure and red hair. She was a comely woman, out here all alone.

"What's your name?" he asked.

"Helen," she answered. "Helen Hardin. And yours?" she asked.

"I was named Bear," he said.

"That seems appropriate." She smiled. She was a bit terrified by his leather and guns, but she felt safe under his steady gaze. "You just passing through?"

"Yes ma'am," he answered. The real purpose of his wanderings he would keep to himself. "You know you ought to move into town till your husband gets home. It ain't safe for a woman to be out in the reaches like this."

"My kids would be safer, it's true," she replied. "But this is all we got. A small spread west of Durango. It could be gone if I abandon it."

"It might all be gone if you don't do what's safe for you and your kids," he said.

"Yeah, that thought has been growing on my mind. Emma and Charlie need school and we're stuck out here on hell's 300 acres."

Bear was sympathetic, but he had his own agenda. He fell silent and Helen got up and busied herself with the daily chores.

Bear was tired; she offered him the barn to bed down in and he took her kindly offer. Just a place to be off the trail for a while and shelter for his horse.

The dog, which was part of Helen's family, had become friendly with him, followed him and lay down at his feet and was one with him. That seemed unusual. Bear thought he must be the spirit of his uncle Iwakan, visiting for a while. He lay down in the barn on an old straw stuffed bed that was by the chopping block. He hoped the echoes of gunfire and men screaming in his head did not interrupt his sleep.

The dog barked angrily as Bear came out of a dream. There was something going on up at the house. Bear made sure his guns were loaded, put on his hat, and moved swiftly to swing into the saddle of his horse. He had only loosened the strap and not taken it off. He knew there may be a time that he needed to make a swift break for it.

He rode calmly out of the barn and around the house. There in front of the horse railing he saw two men, scruffy and dirty, but well-armed. One had Helen bent over the railing, arms pinned behind her back, dress pulled up, showing her bare bottom, ready to take his pleasure.

Bear drew and fired so fast they didn't have time to respond. The first man grew a red hole in the front of his head; he didn't feel a thing. The second turned and ran. Bear drew his 45-70 from its sheath, cocked and fired. The man went down in a cloud of dust – dead as he lay.

Helen was in tears, sobbing about being raped.

"Are you alive or dead?" Bear said stiffly. "Pull down your dress, then put your kids and things in the buckboard and get into town now!"

There were two horses. One she hitched to the buckboard. The other was tied up behind.

"There is probably paper on these two men," he told her. "If so, I'll collect the money and split it with you so you can get settled at the Hotel."

They wandered slowly down the dirt road. The blue still sky was like a big jewel over them. The wind began blowing from the south west, light and faint. The clop of the horse's hooves echoed loudly in the silence. Helen pulled the buckboard to a stop and looked back at Bear. Emma and Charlie were asleep in the back of the wagon.

"They would have raped and killed me," she said in a shaky voice. "Thank you for being there."

Bear just looked at her and said, "Let's move along Helen, or we won't reach Durango by night fall."

About 4:30 the sun was westering, and Helen, the kids, Bear, and the bodies, were pulling down a hill to the small town of Durango. People looked with awe at the huge Indian and with pity at Helen, Emma and Charlie. The four of them pulled up in front of a red brick building with a large wooden sign that said 'Sheriff.' Bear dismounted and went in. Sitting behind the desk was a potbellied older man. He had a leather vest on and a star on his left chest.

He eyed Bear with disgust. "What'd you want, Boy?"

Bear was used to that kind of derision from white authority; he thought it was beneath him to respond.

"Got two kills here," he said. I'm Bear Itaxsca, bounty hunter, caught these two raping a white woman. I did your job."

The Sheriff was angry that an Indian should address him that way, but he caught sight of the gleaming pair of Colt 36's and the Navy .44 stuck in his belt and had second thoughts.

"What's your number?" asked the Sheriff.

Bear slowly lifted his hat and pulled a piece of paper out.

"Federal Warrant issued 964961865," Bear responded. Each bounty hunter had to be identified by the government to legally hunt men. That was Bear's number, attested by a judge in Fort Smith.

"I may have seen 'em before," the Sheriff said under his breath. "You got the carcasses?"

"Come take a look," Bear invited him.

The Sheriff rose stiffly out of his chair. He didn't like the idea of some damned Indian as a federal law dog. They'd had trouble with Indians and to him it wasn't natural.

He followed Bear out to the horses and looked at the two bodies.

"Yeah, that's old Smiley Crocker," he said right away. He moved to the other body, "Angus Watson." he said. "Let me go look at the Wanteds." He hobbled back into the office as Bear waited in the street.

"You got a fair piece coming," the Sheriff said. "$1,000 for Angus and $2,500 for Smiley. We been hunting them for a coon's age."

"Good," answered Bear. "Give $1,250 to the lady in the wagon over there and $2,250 to me."

It took the bank a good deal of time to get this man his money. The warrants were old and they had to telegraph Fort Smith for verification. In the end, Bear planted $1,250 in Helen Hardin's hand.

"That ought to do you till your husband gets back."

"How can I thank you?" she said with a small voice.

"No need, Ma'am." Bear said. It's been a long time since he had had a woman, but this was not the time or place for that.

"Take care of the kids," he said flatly.

II

Bear paid a visit to the Sheriff before he left. "Any major paper?" he asked.

"You did a good job for Mrs. Hardin." The Sheriff said. "Wouldn't think that'd be like...."

"Like an Indian?" Bear interrupted. "Look Mister, I don't like your White ass just as much as you don't like my Red one. Let's not pretend! But I'm good at my job, unlike you at yours. I bring 'em in; you pay me. I'm not here to sit at your table or go to bed with your daughter. I'm here to get the guys you can't. So let's just do business, O.K?"

The Sheriff looked angry and probably would have shot Bear between the eyes if he thought he was a good enough shot. "Fair enough," he said stiffly. "I got one that's been raiding the new copper mine payroll over Scottsdale way. Apache Joe Obisano! The Anaconda Company has $10,000 on his head. Here's the flyer." The sheriff shoved it across the desk at Bear.

"That's a lot of cash," Bear said flatly. "He must be a real bad man."

"Real bad," repeated the sheriff. "When they find your body where do you want it sent?"

Bear just looked hard at the White Eyes and said to himself, 'You would have no idea!'

Bear folded up the flyer and stood up. The metal gleamed off his well-tended weapons; his straight well-muscled frame gave the impression of strength. He stared at the prejudiced potbellied Sheriff and said, "If I can get him, I will."

Bear stepped into the rising sun looking square at the shining orb, feeling the mountain air blow in his face. He had spent the night at the hotel, paying up front because he was an Indian. The resentment he felt for these Whites was unmeasurable, but he realized it was his people that let them win. They let them in by having a tribal circle and insulating themselves, the tribe not realizing that all those outsiders were not enemies. He witnessed many tribes become divided and fall. He would not make that mistake. He knew the White man's weakness – money. Now they would pay him to do what was beyond most of them, having the courage to hunt men!

"Apache Joe!" he said to himself. It shouldn't be hard to find him. He didn't seem to cover his tracks that well. Bear started by paying a visit to the newspaper in Durango. He would find all the information they had on Joe's crimes. "That'll give me a good idea where to look for him."

The newspaper owner operator was surprised that an Indian would have the presence of mind to study on this man.

Bear looked over copies of the Durango Golden Gazette and it seemed Apache Joe had been busy all the way from Durango to Scottsdale, Arizona Territory. The photo that identified him looked more like a Comanche Chief called Dull Knife, and Bear suspected there was no real photo of the Apache Joe Obisano. The only way to get a start on this was to find Apache Joe's woman. He suspected a central cabin or hogan somewhere within riding distance of Scottsdale. That meant trekking south along the mountains - high and wild country.

He had been about three days out along the Apache trail when he ran into some Native Americans. They claimed to be Comanche, but he suspected them to be Crow soldiers.

"Hai! He hailed them. "Mitakuye oyasin!"

"Mitakuye oyasin!" said the lead brave. "You dress like a White man! What is your tribe?"

Bear caught his eye as the band closed in around him. "I am a bounty hunter looking for an outlaw for money. What do you know?"

"I would not tell you anything!" The other Native spat.

"That's too bad," Bear smiled. His voice was friendless and bore the ear mark of a threat.

"You dress like a White man, but you speak Crow. Who are you?"

"Bear Itaxsca," he said, his eyes unblinking and steady.

"I have heard of you," said the warrior with guarded suspicion. "What if I kill you and put your hair on my spear?"

"You talk big for a man who's afraid," Bear replied. "You can scream the victory song after you have got my hair. Make your move warrior!"

The other man eyed him cautiously. "You are brave...but foolish."

"I have no time for caution," Bear said. "I follow the trail of Apache Joe. What do you know of him?"

The band of men looked at one another and slowly said, "None of the tribes have a thing to do with him. We know nothing of him."

"As it should be, Warrior. That's good," Bear replied. "Honorable men shouldn't have to do with such as Apache Joe. Well Warrior," Bear added, "I've got places to go and people to see. You going to take my scalp or sit around and talk about it." Bear goaded his horse in the ribs and suddenly pulled out his 36 Colt. Horse had jumped so that the barrel rested on the warrior's forehead.

"Now all you nice guys might get me if you're fast, but this man's head I will turn into a canoe in an instant," he said calmly. "Make your choice."

They all backed off to let him through. Their eyes blazed, but they could see he was no one to bluff.

He rode on, none the richer for the experience.

III

Bear was five days out of Durango, headed South on the search for the criminal Apache Joe Obisano. Sometimes the day was so still he could hear the spirits around him. He knew they were there and only his Whiteman's teaching let him ignore them. He had a purpose, what that was, had yet to be made clear. He had been given a warrior's talent. What else would come, he knew in time that Wakan Tanka, Great Grandfather Spirit, would show him.

He made fire and laid out his bed roll with a blanket down the middle. Then he carefully chose a place just up the hill to put his hammock up between two sheltered trees, a trick he had learned in the army when Rebs would empty their weapon into your bed roll just to say good night.

It was about three in the morning when he heard some footsteps outside his camp. He swung out of the hammock, pulling his twin 36's out and ready.

"Hai," he said softly.

"Hai," answered a female voice from outside the camp.

"Make yourself known," Bear said.

Into the light of the embering fire stepped a small woman. She had a small fox beside her who was her familiar and she was dressed in typical Crow garb, long dress, moccasins, hair parted and braided on the side. She was old.

"Mitakuye Oyasin," he said.

"Hai," answered the old woman. "Hetche tuelo. Are you the son of Itaxsca?" she asked.

"In the flesh. And you?" he answered her.

"I am Wakan Win." she said.

"And how do you know me?" Bear asked.

"I was there at your birth. I was there at your death when you went to serve the long knives."

"Well mother," he said, trying to ignore the chill that crept up his back. "Come to the fire and be welcome in my camp. "What is it that you seek?" he asked after she had squatted on her heels next to the fire.

"You," she said curtly. "You were dead to your family because they never heard from you, and I knew it was not so. You must go and find them."

"Do you know where they are?" Bear asked as he handed her a large piece of jerky. She sucked on it merrily, smiling for the gift of food.

"Eagle Mountain," she said.

"I've never heard of that place," he replied, yet he knew where it was.

"North," she said and got up. She seemed to fade into the early morning darkness. He looked around but knew she had been a sending spirit. When he was done with Apache Joe he would look for his family. He had been alone long enough.

IV

The wind blew cold from the East as the arc of the sun crept over the mountains. It was early June and the traveling would be easy today. Bear had taken the time to clean his weapons and sharpen the knives he owned. He marveled at how easy the new cartridge cylinders made it to keep your guns clean. His face was drawn into an unemotional mask as he thought of the road ahead. 'Sixty-five more miles to Scottsdale,' he thought. 'Better to keep both eyes peeled.'

The slow clop of his horse's hooves on the ground. Of a sudden the small birds tweeting in the trees around him grew silent.

"We got company Horse," he said under his breath. Suddenly from behind him came the slim shape of the dog he had befriended at Helen's. The dog came and sat on the ground beside the horse. "Couldn't stand that town, huh?" Bear said playfully. "O.K. You can be my ears and eyes."

The dog immediately took point on the trail. All was right with the world again. Dog did not have a playful nature. He seemed to be all business and he had attached himself to Bear; they were a pack now.

About six more miles down the trail Bear smelled a campfire in the distance. His ears started to burn as they did when danger threatened. 'Must be getting close,' he thought. "Dog!" he said, "Lay back!"

The dog obeyed his command as though he understood each word and hung close to the right heel of the horse. They rode slowly towards the men encamped by the trail. Bear could have gone around and avoided them altogether, but something told him it was time he approached them; he needed information.

"Hello the camp," he shouted. He was about three hundred yards from their camp perimeter. "Can I come in?"

"Come ahead, Stranger," was the reply.

Bear walked his horse slowly into the camp taking careful note of every detail, where the horses were, where the hands of the four men were, who held a gun, and the faces of the men.

"Cha cho jah," he said in Crow.

"Cha cho jah," the stranger replied, but he was not Native. The skinny mean looking man seemed to be the leader.

"Are you running a cold camp or is there coffee?" Bear asked.

"There is coffee; come ahead."

Bear could hear Dog growl in his deep throat. "Dog! He gets excited you know. Strangers make him uneasy."

"Well, you keep him on a short leash," said one of the men. "Can't stand a mean dog."

"Oh, he's alright," Bear said as he grinned. "What news on the trail to Scottsdale? Anything I should watch for?"

"Not much," said the skinny man. "There' a slide on up the trail about ten miles, some wolves out, nothing much."

"Whew! That's good." Bear replied.

There was a strange wordless silence. It seemed a tense situation.

"What's your line?" asked the skinny man.

"I hunt," said Bear.

"You hunt what?"

"I hunt men," smiled Bear. He had a hunch that more than one of these men had paper on them, but more importantly, he thought they belonged to the Apache Joe gang.

"Whoa, partner, that's one hell of a job you got."

"Well, you fellas aren't on my list," he laughed. "So rest easy."

Bear gave the crew a once over, the skinny guy with wall eyes, a chubby man that had a buffalo robe coat. This man had blue eyes that would not look you in the eye, and the other two. They were plain, non-descript sorts, all packing two or more pistols; they all had worn down boots.

"Mind us asking who you're after?" asked the skinny man.

"Not at all," said Bear calmly. "Joe Obisan, known as Apache Joe."

There was a silence and they looked nervous. "You know where he's at?" asked Bear.

"Them's pretty high stakes, stranger," said the skinny man.

"Well you gotta aim high in this life to succeed," Bear said jokingly. "When you see him, tell him Bear Itaxsca is on his trail."

"We got nothin' to do with that fella," the skinny fellow insisted.

"Thanks for the coffee," Bear said as he got up to leave. He figured those four were men were planted to find out his purpose. They were too scared to want to take him in a gunfight, but they fit his purpose in letting Apache Joe know who was hunting him.

"Have a well day, a hetche tuelo."

They eyed him hard as he went to his horse; Dog growled and followed close on his heels. He figured Apache Joe would know about him by noon. He was ready for a visit.

V

Bear traveled on, slowly keeping both eyes peeled. He knew he was offering his back to a ruthless criminal hoping he would take his shot. Flushing Joe Obisan out was the first order of business. Bear knew he wouldn't make a move until Bear hit Apache Joe where he lived – in his manner of livelihood and his wallet.

The trail wandered in and out, up and down, until finally the smoke and haze that hung over Scottsdale could be seen in the distance. The high mountain desert was dry and punctuated with small patches of Lodgepole pine and Peyote cactus in rough bits along the trail. Finally after a slow uphill pull the little berg of Scottsdale appeared in the valley below. The two score of buildings were huddled together along a small creek that ran down from the snowy heights behind. 'A cruddy, dirty little village,' Bear thought.

As he and his horse and dog came to the edge of town he saw a sign. It read: "No Redskins or Chinese allowed here."

Bear had seen these epithets before; he had always chosen to ignore them.

He rode up to the bar and hotel. Copper Creek Inn, the sign said. He dismounted and walked into the bar. His boots rang hollow as a silence fell from the few people there.

"Ya'll can't be in here," said the bartender nervously.

Bear didn't say a word. He just drew his Navy Colt and laid it on the bar, cocked. "I'll be needing a room." he said flatly.

The bartender got his drift and went to the key board, removing key number 22. "That'll be fifty cents a day," he said. Bear put down a $5.00 gold piece and said, "I'll be leaving when that's done. Where is the Sheriff's office?"

"Can't miss it, 'bout five doors down." said the barkeep.

Bear took his gun, holstered it and scooped up the keys to #22. He went down to the Sheriff's office and walked in straight and proud.

The Sheriff looked him up and down with an air of disgust. "Itaxsca?" he asked.

Bear nodded. "Sheriff up to Durango wired me you'd be comin'. You here to get Joe?"

"Seems to be the general knowledge," Bear stated.

"News travels fast. Besides, I don't think Apache Joe will let you live that long."

"You know the man?" Bear asked.

"Know of him," said the Sheriff. "Others have come. They are all buried up on boot hill."

Bear took out a $20 gold piece and threw it on the desk.

"That'll pay for my demise, just throw me on a fire and spread the ashes."

The Sheriff looked at him with an angry eye.

"Room 22, if you need to talk to me some more."

He turned and walked into the dusk.

Bear felt the animosity around him. The Apache had been cruel to these townspeople and to them all Natives were 'injuns'. They didn't know one person from the other. He didn't care.

Room 22 was a dismal little cubical with a table, chairs and a low bed. Bear thought laying his bedroll out would be safer. The mattress was crawling with bed bugs. The room hadn't even been swept for a decade it seemed. None the less, he settled down to clean his ordinance. First Bear whetted his stone and sharpened his knife. Then he methodically took apart, cleaned and put back together each of his weapons. First the .45-70. He oiled and scrubbed it until it looked brand new. Bear was careful to keep his weapons in working order at all times. He was an Indian and he knew that was not a safe position in this town.

He was pushing 26 years of age and with that damned war he had learned one important lesson: never think you're safe and never trust anyone. He allowed his mind to drift a while and his thoughts went back to Helen whom he had rescued from the rapist. She had a fine ass, he thought, it was a shame to pass something up as good as that if it was freely offered. "Ah well," he sighed. "You don't shit where you eat. Women should be in the right place and the right time."

All finished, he settled down for some rest. The dog was in the corner. He locked the window with a stick and put a chair under the door knob. Not totally safe, but it would do. He kept his guns loaded, one under his bedroll.

As Bear took pleasure in cleaning his weapons, he also took pleasure in planning his next move to get Apache Joe, alive if possible, then to the Sheriff in Scottsdale. The mystery of who Joe Obisan was, though, plagued him. He seemed a ghost that was very successful in robbing banks, stages, burning, pillaging farms, etcetera.

It was about midnight and he heard the dog growl. There were footsteps outside his door and he didn't think it was the drunken whores that lived in the hotel.

"It's locked," he heard a low voice say. That god damned Injun needs a lesson."

"Yeah, we need to take him apart."

Bear knew he would be getting a visitation. It happened everywhere. You could never intrude on the white man's world without a struggle.

Bear sashed his guns quickly, pulled on his boots, ready to settle this. He got up and removed the chair and opened the door.

"You gentlemen looking for me?" he asked.

"There he is!" shouted one of them, a scruffy looking miner. "Get him!" First one, then two more came at Bear. He caught the first one on the button with his right and down went the man. He pushed the other two down the stairs to his right. The other was a cool looking man with his gun drawn. He spoke slowly. "I hear you're looking for me" he said. It was Apache Joe. He was a man of medium build, with sharp eyes and the calmness of knowing he had successfully trapped his quarry. He also was a Crow Indian.

"Cho da jah," said Bear, surprised.

"Cho da jah," said Joe. "Now why do you hunt me?"

"Ten thousand dollars," said Bear.

"I've gone up, Brother," Joe said. "It's nice to know they value my scalp that high. You've been gone a long time," Joe said. "It's good to see you."

Bear was more than surprised. "Joseph Itaxsca," he muttered. "So you are Apache Joe?"

"In the flesh," he replied, and holstered his gun.

"Brother," Bear said with wonderment in his eyes. "How came you to this? I am duty bound to take you in." said Bear. "What has happened to you?"

An angry look came over Joseph Itaxsca's face. "When you left the Long Knives, the soldiers came to the village. They told us we couldn't live free, hunt where they had, and that we belonged to the Federal government. Pah!" he spat. "They set up settlers in towns on the Buffalo graze. They said we could make money by whoring our women out to the soldiers. I found a different way. I took from them!"

"If you turn yourself in, I can buy you out in a year or two." Bear uttered the words but he knew it wouldn't be so.

"No, Brother," Joseph said. "You will have to catch me, and that won't be easy. Good bye."

Joseph opened the door behind him, shut it and locked it faster than Bear could react.

Bear kicked in the door, guns drawn, but all he found was a couple in the middle of having sex, and an open window. Bear glanced at the man humping away on the woman, shook his head and left them to it.

VI

Knowing that he was hunting his brother changed the complexion of this hunt. He was faced with two choices, one, to just get on his horse and turn back North to find his family at Whiskey Mountain, or two, hunt Joseph down and kill him. That's what he would have to do. Make the hard choice.

He made his way back to room 22 with a heavy heart. It was the last thing he would have suspected; his brother turned outlaw. He knew suddenly that he was not alone. Had Joseph come to settle up, a change of heart? A small knock on his door and he pulled his .36, moving cautiously to answer.

"Who is it?" Bear said. There was no answer. He jerked the door open and there stood the small old Indian woman who had visited him at his camp. She just hobbled in and sat down on the floor next to the window. The small red fox that was her familiar trotted in behind her.

"Wakan Win," Bear said. "What brings you into white man's town?"

"You," she croaked. "And your brother Joseph."

"Well, Mother, there is no passing this one by, he said. "I must track him down, catch him or kill him."

"Do you not fear becoming a witch?" she asked.

"I am duty bound. I have taken the contract to find him." Bear was sagging at the shoulders with the prospect of shooting Joseph down.

"Hmm," Wakan win mused. "It is time for The Itaxsca to get involved."

"What can our grandfather do?" Bear asked.

She didn't say another word. She motioned for him to give her another piece of jerky and she sat there sucking on it.

Bear got his coat and hat. When he turned around, Wakan win was gone. He wondered what she meant by "The Itaxsca." It would be his grandfather who had been mighty in medicine, but he died long ago when Bear was a boy. It was crazy. He shrugged his shoulders. It was time for the hunt.

VII

Bear packed his things. Dog and he went to the stable where he was boarding Horse. It seemed odd the way Horse was reacting to him. He hummed a little song and patted the neck of the animal while he saddled him.

"Ho boy," he said gently. "I am not the enemy. Be calm."

The horse eventually licked his lips and bowed his head. Saddled, Bear swung easily aboard and they were off. Scottsdale was not the place anymore.

"What would my brother do?" he mused. "I would have me watched to see what I would do." As he headed back north out of town he suspected eyes were on his every move.

"Ok, Horse, let's lose 'em," he said as he spurred the animal into a good gallop. Straight up to the knot of trees above the road. He rode into the brush and waited.

Soon three men, sort of raggedy types, came careful like up the hill. They approached the knot of trees looking every which way for signs of Bear's passing.

"I am here." He said quietly."

"Oh my god, Jesus!" said the leader. "You scared ten years off my life!"

"Why do you follow me?" Bear said.

"Some guy, big Indian fella, gave us $20 to see which way you went.

"Why is my direction of such interest?" asked Bear.

"Dunno," said the leader, "But we was to telegraph this fella at Apache Wells and tell him."

"Okay," said Bear. "you've done your job. Here's twenty more," he flipped a $20 gold piece in his direction. "Tell him north, towards Durango."

"Much obliged," said one of the other three.

"Now get and do your job," said Bear.

"Apache Wells," he mused. "That's east and north, a low water stage stop. Nothing much out that way. I wonder?"

Bear didn't spend much time deliberating. He knew Joseph would have to go there to get to the telegraph to find out what Bear was doing. It seemed a lonely fitting place for two brothers to strive against one another.

The trail to Apache Wells was a hard one, low and rugged through some of the worst desert in the land. Bear did not like desert.

Horse clopped along and the days went by uneventfully. Nights were worse because there were no trees to hang a hammock. The only advantage he had was Dog. Dog was a curious individual. He was not a lap pup, he hunted for himself and was ever up for a treat from Bear.

"What do you know?" Bear asked his companion, "I think our spirits are linked somehow." The dog just looked at him as if he was crazy and lay down by the fire.

He was 28 miles from Apache Wells. Bear was parched, and his butt was road heavy in the saddle. He had given most of his water to Horse and Dog; he had gone without himself. It had been almost 120 miles from Scottsdale and finally he approached his destination. Bear could see smoke from the cooking stoves in the distance. He reached down and got the canteen and took a mouthful of water. "Better get alert," he told himself.

It was another five hours until he got there, the small stagecoach stop, bar, and the corrals in back. There were some outlying buildings and a barn or two. The buildings were gathered around an oasis in the desert. The water from the mountains had pushed up here in the middle of the desert just to help travelers.

Bear walked his horse into the open space in front of the stagecoach stop.

"Joseph Itaxsca!" He shouted. Out of the saloon came six men. The last of them was Joseph Itaxsca.

"Well brother, you made it." Joseph sneered. It was fast. Guns were drawn and everyone started firing at Bear. Bear hit the ground, twin 36s blazing. First one and then the other went down under his fire. When he cocked and fired there was a cry of pain. He took one bullet that grazed his upper shoulder and he winced with the pain. Bear rose on one knee to examine the damage he'd done. Then all was silent. Five men lay on the ground dead or dying. Joseph sat down and glared at his brother.

"You're going to have to kill me." Joseph said breathlessly. "That'll make you a witch. You want to be a witch?" He was referring to an old Navajo tradition that killing a family member made you a witch, a doer of evil.

"I don't wanna kill you," Bear said. "I want you to come to justice.

There was a bright flash of light. Thunder rolled from a clear blue sky, and it knocked Bear down. There between them stood a figure that seemed to materialize out of thin air. Bear heard the sudden intake of breath from Joseph.

"The Itaxsca!" Joseph said with fear. Bear looked at the figure forming and it seemed to have come from a long way away. When it came into focus he recognized the strong gaunt features of his grandfather. He had been mighty in medicine for the Crow People and his word had been law for over fifty years.

At his side was the diminutive woman Wakan Win, her fox cringing at her ankle.

"Brothers" a huge voice said. The depth and volume was so large it nearly knocked one over to hear it. The Itaxsca stood between the two men, glittering, sparks flying in the air.

"How come you to this?" the Itaxsca questioned.

Bear just bowed his head.

"Bear," said the Itaxsca, "I know you. You were ever the hero, the one who made wrongs right. Come to me my grandson."

Though Bear was afraid, he went to him and the Itaxsca touched him.

"Your heart is good; it is clean."

"No grandfather," Bear wept. "I have done great sin. I fought and killed other men. They had families and loved ones and I took them away.

"Much must be sacrificed in War." said the Itaxsca. "I can see your purpose."

The Itaxsca turned to Joseph. "Come here grandson."

"No," Joseph shouted back. "I can hear you good enough from where I stand."

"I would touch you so that I will know."

"You can go to Hell!" Joseph shouted.

The glittering figure of Itaxsca turned toward Joseph and held out his hand. He folded his hand into a clenched fist and Joseph came flying off the steps of the saloon into his grasp.

"No!" screamed Joseph as his body started to wither. It crumbled like dust around the fist of the Itaxsca, and all that was left was a beating heart in the Itaxsca's hand. There was a flash and the heart turned into a bright jewel in his hand.

"Be at peace, grandson." His voice boomed.

The Itaxsca turned to Bear and his intense eyes held him, seeing to the depths of his soul.

"You have much to do," he said. "Know that I am always with you. Mitakuye oyasin."

The Itaxsca stepped back into the light that surrounded him. He grew smaller and farther away until the blazing light encompassed him. Then he was gone.

Wakan Win stood there, her fox marking her leg in nervous anticipation.

"These," she said, pointing to the bodies that littered the square, "should provide paper enough for you. Take you grandfather's advice, she went on, "Do what you must do and live the life you were given." She turned to walk away and Bear needed to know, "Who are you?" He asked.

Wakan Win turned, her eyes bright in the sunlight. "Do you not know your own Mother, son? Come and find me on Eagle Mountain. I am there." She walked away, getting smaller as she went. There was a shadow that the saloon cast. She walked into it. She was gone.

Bear sat on the saloon steps, his heart still beating fast, trying to make sense of the events that had just occurred. He had been touched by the other side and chills ran up and down his back. He somehow was not afraid of The Itaxsca, his paternal Grandfather. It was a mystery, but the key lay in that diminutive woman, Wakan Win. She was not his mother. What did she mean?

Soon people began to poke their heads out into the square.

"That was some gunfight, mister!" said an old crusty bar keep. "Ain't seen a gun handled like that in a long time. What's your handle?"

Bear looked at the five bodies and at the bar keep.

"Bear," he said. "Bear Itaxsca."

<h3 style="text-align:center">VIII</h3>

It was morning and the sun shone brightly, the still air and blue sky seemed to make everything serene and peaceful. The mayor of Apache Wells had taken charge to get the bodies off the street and Bear spent the night in the saloon, room #11. The mayor had moved the whore that did business there out, and Bear seemed to collapse on the bed. He fell into a deep sleep and didn't wake until late on this fine still morning.

There came a knock on the door. "Mr. Itaxsca?"

"Yes," he answered. "What is it?"

"Mayor Duncan would like to talk to you. Are you decent?"

"Yes, yes. I'll be right down," he replied. He knew there'd be business to take care of.

"Dog?" he called. There was a whimper from the corner and Dog came out wanting affection from Bear.

"Well, I guess we gotta go justify all this." He said to the dog.

Bear and Dog went out the door and down the stairs. There were about twenty people out front curious to see the man that brought down Apache Joe and his crew.

"We all come out today to thank you, Mr. Bear." said an aging woman. She was in a flower print blue dress, her graying hair was pulled back in a bun.

"Them scoundrels been using the Well as their private getaway for about five years. It was not a good time. Now it's over." She said. "Thank you."

Bear just nodded.

"We took the liberty of telegraphing the Marshall's office in Durango about them you killed. They all got paper on 'em," said the mayor. "And you're entitled to quite a sum. Said they couldn't pay for Joe without a body, but the others, brother you got at least 12,000 Yankee dollars coming to you!"

"Good," Bear said. "I'll take the money. Telegraph it to the bank in Durango. That's where I'm headed."

Bear didn't much care about the money. He was still a bit shocked by the lightning in his grandfather's eyes. He hit the northward trail with Horse and Dog and never looked back.

IX

It took him twenty-two days of slow traveling before he came to the Rio Grande Valley, high in the mountains. The river swift and blue green color like it hadn't collected all that mud and silt yet. The aspens were all turning yellow and the leaves were all burned orange by the summer sun. he breathed in the pure air of the high mountains and calm came over his mind.

Dog caught a rabbit last night and brought it to Bear. They shared it over the campfire and this morning they felt better going into town.

"Wonder if that mayor ever wired my money." Bear said to Dog. Dog said nothing.

An hour later Horse's hoofs beat a slow walk on the streets of Durango. After all the country Bear had covered it seemed a fine and familiar place. He wondered about the woman he had helped, "Helen Hardin." Was she still there in the hotel?

His boots clonked on the wood sidewalk after tying Horse up to the rail and loosening his saddle. He opened the door to the saloon and walked in. Who do you think was behind the bar serving drinks? It was none other than Helen Hardin. She looked steady at Bear and before he could say a word she blurted out, "What took you so long?" Bear's eyebrow lifted and he was surprised when she ran out from behind the bar, ran over to him, and wrapped her arms around him in a giant hug. It felt good.

Helen looked at him and said, "You been through a lot."

Bear just smiled. He didn't do well with women.

She hustled around, got him a huge steak and home fries to eat. Then she sat with him.

"We found out Fred wasn't comin' home," she said after a while. "He'd gone all the way to Denver and ran across trouble; they brought his body home to bury."

"I'm sorry," Bear said. He was feeling tender towards this woman. He wanted to reach out and crush her to him, but he had other concerns. Still, it felt good to be mothered for a while. He looked at her and said, "My room is #11. If you would like to stay with me tonight it will be alright."

Helen looked at him. "My, you are a direct man," she said.

Bear made sure his money was in the bank and Horse was stabled. He went to the hotel, room 11, and went through his routine - stick in the window, chair against the door. He was laying on the bed when he heard the tiniest knock. He grabbed his .36, cocked the hammer and said, "Who's there?"

A small voice answered, "It's me, Helen."

Bear opened the door and she came in.

"I need to be with you," she said. "I know this is brazen, but I just need you."

She slipped her blouse off and wriggled out of her pants. She fell naked into his arms and they fell back onto the bed. It was the first woman Bear had had since the end of the War. It was good.

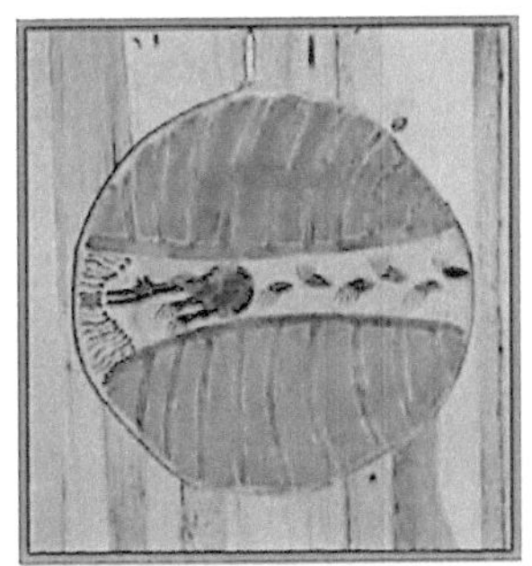

The Birth of Bear Itaxsca

It was one of those still October mornings, the yellow grass swaying gently with the wind, the nip of first frost biting the air. The sun seemed to rise reluctantly on the Shoshone River, and Blue Knife Itaxsca waited outside the teepee; his second son was about to enter the world. Blue Knife stared at the arc of the rising sun and from within the teepee came the cry of a newborn baby. Blue Knife heaved a sigh of relief. Marsilla, his wife, had been pregnant with this child forever it seemed, and now he had come.

Blue Knife pulled back the flap of the teepee, "Have you born me a son?" he asked.

"Yes, my husband," came the gentle reply from Marsilla. Blue Knife took the newborn from her arms; the old Crow midwife Bahalli chattered about being careful. The baby screamed loud to the rising sun, wriggling in his father's arms.

"Bear, I shall name you," Blue Knife said as he offered the child to Wakan Tanka. "Bear Itaxsca you shall be called."

It was the fifteenth of October 1842, the Shoshone River but a trickle waiting for the fall rain, but life was good for Blue Knife Itaxsca. Soon they would hunt the Yellowstone for Buffalo before moving South to the winter hunting grounds. Blue Knife breathed deeply the morning air and handed the child back to Bahalli. She had helped in the delivery of over one hundred Crow babies. Marsilla was glad to have her.

The other child, Joseph, was four years older. He peered wide-eyed around the edge of the teepee. 'What was going on?' he thought. He didn't at all like his father paying so much attention to this new thing. His face was dark with suspicion.

Marsilla carried Bear in a rack, but she did not bind him in. "Better he be free," she said to herself. She went singing about her chores and her life. It was good. The only thing wrong, she felt, was the Itaxsca. He was a powerful medicine man, Blue Knife's father. He frightened her, and he would be around to visit soon.

"Why does he frighten you so much?" Blue Knife asked her.

"It's like he can see me," she said, "the deep inside I only show to you."

"Hah!" Blue Knife laughed. "I hope it's not a wicked plot to scalp me and take my bow and arrows."

Then it was winter and time to move from the Shoshone River to the lowlands closer to the Yellowstone. The winter seemed less hard there. There were buffalo, and the deer grew fat in that valley.

The village prayed to Wakan Tanka and the four winds. The last to leave was the Itaxsca and his family. Winter blew cold from the north and the bitter winds seemed to push them from the valley.

"It is time to go," Blue Knife told Marsilla, who was reluctant to leave. The Shoshone River Valley had been a safe place for her. She knew the weather would drive them though, and there was Bear to think of.

"Wizopeyata [North Wind} is not pleased," said Blue Knife. "Let's get out of here."

There were fourteen families making the trek. Bear, the new member of the tribe, was intent on nursing from

Marsilla. The men dragged their travois over the Eagle Mountain, down into the Yellowstone. Blue Knife and the Itaxsca had gone ahead on horseback to secure and bless the valley. The families came after. Twenty or so warrior rode guard just in case they encountered Lakotas. They did not want to fight with the Lakota when the women and children were with them. Each family had a guardian to watch over them on the journey. Blue Knife had chosen White Pony to be his family's guardian. He was an able warrior of eighteen summers and had very powerful medicine for such a young brave.

Blue Knife and the Itaxsca secured their camp near the big geyser that shot up every hour. The smoke and steam kept the snow away and the grass remained green even in the dead of winter. The geese crowded the landscape and on the far plain they had seen buffalo and deer. It was a paradise to hunt there and all you had to watch for were the Arapaho. They were mean Indians, with no respect for other tribes and considered the Yellowstone theirs, while the Crow also considered it theirs. They often fought over this territory.

The Itaxsca blessed the camp and his wives set up his teepee on the top of a hill overlooking the small valley. He was the Eagle Mountain holy man, well known for his medicine, and he was Bear's grandfather. He was old, but still hale. Tribal members whispered to one another that he could call down the lightning upon his enemies. He was tall for a Crow Native, about six-foot one inch, and his muscular body seemed twisted like and old root, tough and weather worn.

"The valley is good this year," he would say, "and we will hunt with the spirit of our ancestors." If the Itaxsca said it, it must be true.

It was ten days of travel when finally, Marsilla and the other women and children topped the ridge and started down into the camp. The road had been hard, and Bear was restless; it had been a difficult journey for one so small. Joseph was out of sorts too, just four years and he had learned to swear. "God damned," he cursed in relief. "Finally got here."

"Thank Wakan Tanka {Great Spirit]," Marsilla said. "Do not curse him." She said to young Joseph.

"You know nothing, woman," he said under his breath. Joseph was an angry and disturbed child.

The camp was set up comfortably for the incoming people and Marsilla met Blue Knife at their teepee with a smile; it would be good to feel a strong man in her arms again. Then there was Bear. He wriggled and wanted to be fed. Thus, life went on for Bear and his family, even as the men anticipated the Elk coming into season.

II

Nine years after Bear Itaxsca's birth, he was a strong boy with fire in his eyes, proud and stern. This year though, he would experience sorrow. His grandfather, the Itaxsca, was dying. He lay in his teepee and his clans people were around him, singing his death song; it would not be long.

Suddenly, Blue Knife, Bear's father, appeared from behind the teepee. "You are called for," he said to Bear. "The Itaxsca wants to see you before he goes." Blue Knife's sorrow was apparent, but he was trying hard not to show the signs of weakness that he felt.

Bear followed his father's lead dutifully to the teepee of Grandfather Itaxsca. It was all he could do to drag his feet across the threshold of the open flap.

There, lying on his Buffalo skins was the old Holy Man.

"Come here, Bear," he said weakly. "You have earned your medicine bag." Grandfather took the small leather bag from around his neck and placed it in Bear's outstretched hand. "Honor the Ancestors," he said weakly. "You of all my children have earned the right to wear the medicine of the Ancients."

"Yes, Grandfather," Bear said. He looped the leather thong that held the medicine bag over his head and saw the old man smile. "I go with Wakan Tanka," he whispered. He lay back as his eyes fluttered a little, then he was still. Bear saw a shadow rise up from his body, stretch itself and then fade into the distance; the Itaxsca was dead.

Death was a common experience for the Natives in the 1850's, but the Itaxsca had been the strong Holy man of the tribe and he had been depended on to keep straight with Wakan Tanka. Now they would have to depend on Bahalli, the Itaxsca's third wife, to interpret the ceremonial words and do the ceremonies. She was strong, but on this day, there were tears in her eyes.

The fact that Bear, a nine-year-old boy, now wore the medicine bag of the Itaxsca, was odd to the people; they would reverence him for that, but he was so young.

The Itaxsca was put on a rack high off the ground and open bare to the four winds beyond Eagle Mountain. His spirit would wander freely.

It was a year before Bear got over the experience of the Itaxsca's death. As Bear grew, he hunted with the men. His frame was solid, and he killed his first buffalo in his tenth year.

As the 1850's were fading away, Bear became tall and muscular, the perfect picture of a man by the time he was sixteen. It was at this time that the White men began showing up in great numbers. He had seen them, scruffy types, that came to trade with the Crow, but now whole families came with their wagons. He rode out to greet them.

They seemed afraid of the proud Crow warriors; they were not good at sign language or anything else it seemed to Bear. There was a never-ending stream coming from the East.

Blue Knife held them in contempt but had no objection to their passing through, as long as they were hunting what they needed and then leaving. Bear, on the other hand, was curious about them. They were different, not at all like the Crow. He followed them, watched them when he could, listened to the unusual speech and manners. Bear quickly learned their language and began his own trade with them. They were poor horsemen and stupid hunters, but the one thing they had that he wanted were guns, rifles and pistols.

As time passed, Bear was able to acquire rifles and ammunition for the tribe. By the time he was sixteen the Crow were armed, and hunting was much easier. Bear traded for two bright shiny Colt .36's power and ball, from a man for one buffalo hide. He stuck the guns in his sash, so they would stay put. It seemed to him that they were good for settling arguments.

Bear was also a powerful dancer. Every spring hunt he danced with the people, the Buffalo dance after the first kill and thanked Wakan Tanka for the blessing of bone tools, food and hides to keep the tribe fed and sheltered.

As the days passed Bear had more and more to do with the Whites that crossed their land. One day, as he rode to the camp of the wagon train, he saw a young girl who seemed about thirteen years old. She was running and jumping in the tall grass. It struck him how very beautiful she was. He rode toward her and in Crow, he said, "Cho da cha." She turned around in fright and stared at him.

"Do not be afraid," he said again in English. "You are away from your tribe," he continued. "It is not safe to be a woman out here all alone."

She calmed down and stopped her shaking with panic. "You're an Indian," she said softly.

"Yes. I am a Crow warrior," he answered.

She smiled as she looked up at him. Bear had turned into a magnificent warrior with a straight back and well-muscled all over. "You speak English too," she said.

"Yes," he smiled. "The traders taught me years ago."

"My name is Andrea Andrews," she went on gaily. "It's a beautiful day, is it not?"

"I can smell the North wind today," Bear replied. He felt the tug of her beauty with this White girl. He also felt her innocence. "You should go back to the wagons, Andrea," he said gently. "There are others about that would take you for a slave wife."

She looked worried. "You wouldn't be one of those, would you?"

"No," he laughed. "I have too much to do to bother you. And besides, I have no lodge to take you to. I still lodge with my father."

Andrea heard a faint call from the wagons. "I better go, Mr. Indian. It was nice meeting you."

She turned on her heel and ran back to the wagons. Bear sat still as a statue watching her. In his heart he heard himself say, "That was a rare beauty."

Bear returned daily to the wagon train; he was curious about Andrea. Mostly, the wagon train plodded along several miles a day, stopping longer at water. He knew they would soon come to mountains and the trail that led into the Nez Perce lands. He followed them until they were almost to the mountains and he saw the girl Andrea again.

"Hi there, Mr. Indian." she said to him. His back was turned, and he was startled. He hadn't seen her. He turned his horse to greet her.

"Hello," he replied. "You are out and about again."

"Yeah," she paused. "I was lookin' for you."

"What did you want little one?" he asked.

She didn't say a word. She just reached behind her neck and undid her dress. It fell to the ground and she stood there naked.

"I want you to make love to me." She whispered. "My mother said I should pick the man I want to be with, and I pick you."

Bear was surprised and felt like he should run from this, but she was beautiful. He slid off his horse, threw his blanket down; it was wonderful. She was a virgin, and so was he, but nature took hold. They journeyed to ecstasy.

When they had fulfilled the natural urge that came upon them, Andrea looked Bear in the eyes and saw him clearly. "Oh, my folks would never hold with an Indian, but I think you are the best man God ever created. We are headed to Oregon, but I couldn't leave without letting you love me."

Andrea got up, put her dress on, smiled and said, "Good-bye Mr. Indian. Thank you for loving me."

"My name is Bear," he stated, as if it were a simple fact. She smiled, ran her open hand across his face, then ran away toward the wagons. Bear knew he would never see her again.

III

The winter season at the Yellowstone was almost over. They had survived another year. The tribe was in disarray though, complaining loudly about the White men and their wagons. The parade seemed endless.

"We shouldn't let them cross our land!" shouted Joseph Itaxsca. "They are poison to the air, the earth and water!"

Bear was silent, listening like the owl, until he was ready to speak. "I have seen these White men," He said calmly. "They are hungry for a new start. Much like the Crow were when driven from the plains by the Lakota. I am young, but in my mind, I see the young warriors laying dead on the grass because we do not know how to live with them. The White men, whatever my brother says, are good at one thing, killing. I will not be part of dead Crow littering the prairie. Let us talk to the Whites and become stronger with their knowledge."

"Hah!" shouted Joseph. "I can see no greater strength than 20 warriors burning their wagons and taking their women."

There was a great deal of yelling and screaming from the younger warriors. This was not a formal council where the elders sat in a circle and decided the fate of the people, but rather a loose gathering of warriors. They vented their disgust with the White man.

"They shot a tatonka, striped the back strap and left the rest to rot!" said Black Bow.

"They shoot at us just for fun!" yelled White Elk. "They are evil. Joseph is right; we need to rid the land of them."

"If you do," Bear said, "Five times more will come in their place. And they will crush us like bugs. They are not all bad!"

In the midst of all this turmoil, Blue Knife said, "What are you young men saying? The Whites have done us no harm. They are slow stupid hunters, wasteful and irreverent, but that does not earn them a trip to Wakan Tanka. Let them go!"

"Yes, let them go!" spat out Joseph, "and after they have pissed all over the Yellowstone, we'll thank them! You are blind old men! You are also weak! Are you not the chief and protector of our people?"

"We will not speak of this again," said Blue Knife, "Until a council can be held!" Blue Knife knew that half of his warriors were there, and all were mad as wet sage hens. They would decide what to do about the Whites.

It was ten days before all the leaders of the Crow nation could be called together for a sit down. The Whites were the topic of conversation.

"Many feel anger at their passing through with such arrogance over our lands. What is the answer?" spoke an older chief, Black Nose. "We know there are many more in the East and they are well armed. I do not want to lose more young men and women in a fruitless war."

"Are you afraid?" spoke another, Sharp Bear. "We are Crow, mighty among the mighty. Can we not turn these wagons back?"

"Yes, for today." Spoke Blue Knife. "But tomorrow they will come from the East with more guns and horses than the Crow could gather in a lifetime. Should we not direct them, let them pass and learn from them?"

It was 1861. The Crow were indecisive, and each chief was told to handle it as they would. Bear had watched as the chiefs had gathered. He saw them ride in one and two at a time with their full ceremonial faces on. They were straight and serious beneath their bonnets of eagle feathers.

He wondered if his little dust up disagreement with his brother Joseph caused all this to occur. He knew there had been run-ins with the Whites, and they were, by and large, disrespectful of Wakan Tanka, but he knew that with effort, his people could get along with the Whites. The chiefs smoked with the pipe and danced for three days, and when all had been discussed, Joseph and he were sent for. They were called on to settle the differences between them.

"The two grandsons of the Itaxsca should not strive against each other," said chief Black Nose.

"What do you know?" said Joseph. "You would let the Whites cover you like a blanket of snow in the winter." The chiefs were unmoved by his anger.

"I would say to you, Joseph," said Black Nose. "That there is much room north of Eagle Mountain and you should hunt that way. The Crow will stay south."

Joseph had tears in his eyes. He was being banished for wanting to defend the tribe. 'What a hateful thing to do,' he thought. He ran from the teepee, got on his horse and thundered from the camp. Bear just stood there in silence, his medicine bag burned his chest. The Itaxsca spirit was not pleased.

IV

About this time the Long Knives (soldiers) began to come into Crow land. They were well armed and generally ordered; their people moved about as if they owned all the land. It was said they were fighting a great War in the East with their fellow Whites. Bear was curious and, in his hunting trips he stopped to talk with them.

I can't believe a savage can speak good English." said one belligerent sergeant.

"Who leads you?" asked Bear.

"Well, that would be Captain Morgan." He answered. He made no move to get the captain; he just sat there on his horse, with his hand on his gun. "Those are two pretty nice 36's you have tucked in your sash," he went on. "Who'd ya steal 'em from?"

Bear looked him straight in the eye and said, "It was a good trade. Can I speak with your captain?" He asked.

"Hell no!" spat out the sergeant. "He don't socialize with the likes of you! Be off with you!"

Bear sat silent on his horse. He knew this moron knew nothing. The sergeant was a bully, Bear could see, and did not know how to ask permission to pass on Crow land.

"You are on Crow Land," Bear said. "Your captain needs to ask permission to pass."

"That'll be the day." said the sergeant. He pulled his pistol out and started waving it in Bear's face. "Now why don't you go tell whoever, that the U.S. army is here, and this is the United States. We'll go wherever we want."

Bear was fast. He snatched the gun out of the sergeant's hand, cocked it, and laid the barrel on the man's forehead. The sergeant pissed his pants.

"Now," Bear said, "Take me to your captain, please."

All the rest of the sergeant's men were fumbling for their weapon.

"Good Lord don't shoot!" pleaded the sergeant.

"I won't if you are polite; you are on Crow land."

"Alright, go get the cap'n." the sergeant said.

A couple of the soldiers rode down to the bivouac, a row of tents hastily thrown up for protection against the wind.

Soon a man, neatly dressed, with a sword by his side, came riding up to where Bear held the sergeant, gun barrel still to his head.

"What's all this?" he asked as he rode up. He looked angry behind his bearded face, but also amused.

"I'm Captain Morgan." He said. "The commanding officer of the sixth cavalry in this area."

"Cho da cha," said Bear. "I've been tracking you for days. You are on Crow Land. Please ask permission to pass."

The Captain smiled. "What a fine specimen of a Native American. Who do I ask?" he said.

"Me," answered Bear. "I am the grandson of the Itaxsca, son of Blue Knife, the chief of the Eagle Mountain Crow."

"Well then, I ask," he said. "May we pass through your land?"

Bear smiled, the corners of his mouth just turning up at the edges. "Permission granted." Bear said. I came to talk and smoke with the leader of your group. I was sent to learn of you so that the tribe can understand why you travel through here."

"Well, you better let Mr. McKarcher go then. He's my top sergeant."

Bear twisted the gun, spun it back into the sergeant's holster and rode past him like nothing had happened. McKarcher mumbled something under his breath.

"Will you come to my tent so that we can talk and smoke?" asked Captain Morgan.

"Just you," Bear said. He was not going to be trapped by the soldiers.

"Just me," said Morgan.

They rode together to his tent which was a bit aside from the other tents.

"Mr. Itaxsca," Captain Morgan said. "You are a great warrior."

Bear just looked at him.

"I need great warriors like you."

Bear was still silent as they dismounted and went into the Captain's tent.

"Our country," he went on saying, "Is in a great war with itself." He paused. "Over slavery. Do you know what that is?"

"Yes," said Bear. "It is when one man owns another and forces him to work for him. I have seen Crow women captured by the Lakota, forced to work until they die."

"Then you've got the picture. The Rebs want to enslave people. They think it is the right way to do business. They separated from the United States and are at war with the United States Government."

"Why do you tell me this?" asked Bear.

"There is a great battle to be waged south of here," the Captain continued. "I need warriors like you to help with the fight."

"You are not my people," Bear replied flatly.

"Can you read?" Captain Morgan asked.

"Yes, I can," said Bear.

He and the tribal children had been taught by an old woman named Sarah who had settled west of the Yellowstone with her trapper husband. Bear's mother, Marsilla, thought it a great gift to the Crow children to be able to read. Bear had taken to it like a duck to water. He remembered Sarah kindly as he responded to the Captain. "Yes, yes I can read."

"Then take a look at these," said Captain Morgan. In front of Bear he laid out books with tin types of slaves - their terrible condition. And the women with deep whip scars on their bare backs.

The subtitles were, "Slaves of the Odell Plantation," and "Mac Carthy's Girls." The deep look of hopelessness in the slaves' eyes spoke to Bear and he wanted to rage against these barbarians.

Captain Morgan said then, "These are the few that I can show you. But this is why we must fight and win this war."

"How does this affect the Crow?" asked Bear, pulling himself back to his senses.

"The Crow live free," said Captain Morgan. "If these Grey men prevail, they would enslave your tribe and every other tribe they could find. That's why I need fighters like you to help defeat them.

Bear knew the traps the Whites set for the Red man; he was not unfamiliar with their guile.

"I would fight for you," he said. "If my father, Chief Blue Knife, allows it. But, I am my own person. I do what I can and no more."

Bear rose and walked out of the tent to his horse as Captain Morgan followed. "I will return with the answer."

Bear gracefully leapt upon the back of his horse and rode towards his village.

"That will be my greatest soldier," said Captain Morgan to himself.

V

Bear rode slowly back to the village. He was thinking of how to ask his father for permission to fight for the Whites.

"It is struggle against Slavery," he said to himself. "Even if the Captain is false with the Crow people, this slavery is real. I have seen the Lakota and the Arapaho work slaves until they died." Though he had never met a Black man, he knew slavery was unjust and a worthy battle. He rode slowly down the slope to the village that was nestled in the Shoshone River Valley. He could see the smoke from the cooking fires and hear the dull thud of horses' hooves as they were ridden by the braves. It was dinner time, and all was quiet.

He came to his father's tee pee and dropped the horse's reins so it could run free. His horse would come back at a whistle from Bear.

He pulled back the entrance flap and saw his mother, Marsilla, and his father, eating buffalo stew.

"Just in time, Son," his mother said. "Have you eaten?"

"No," Bear said. "This is buffalo stew?"

"You know it is," she replied with a smile.

His father looked at him with narrowed eyes. "The Wind tells me you have been talking to the Whites, Son." He said. "What is it that they say?"

"They say there is a great war in the east and south," replied Bear. "I talked with a Captain Morgan. He showed me tintypes of Black men and women in slavery."

"And what is that to the Crow?" Blue Knife's voice was stern.

Bear paused, considering his words carefully. "He wants me to join the Blue Coats, Father, and fight the men in Grey for the slaves' freedom."

"That is nothing to the Crow," his father said. "We have enemies enough right here in our own lands."

"Yes," Bear said. "But the captain says, and I believe him, that if the Grey men prevail, they will enslave all."

"I have not seen, though I have heard, about these Grey men," said Blue Knife. "They did not seem any worse than the soldiers you speak with, but the Whites all have...agendas."

"You will not go and fight for them!" shouted Marsilla. "I do not waste my Son on someone else's war!"

"Mother, the cause is just," said Bear. She turned her back on him. "You are a man. Do what you will. But I will not see you until you stop this nonsense about fighting for the Whites."

Blue Knife looked at her and nodded his head. "She is right, you are a man. It is not fit for you to ask permission. You must follow your own trail."

"Now sit down and eat some stew." His father smiled at Bear. He knew Bear would go and he knew that as man, and the carrier of the Itaxsca's medicine bag, he must strive with his own conscience and walk his own trail."

The wind blew cold on his face as he walked his horse to his own teepee across the river. He mounted at the ford and when he reached the dwelling he tethered the animal for the night on a pony line. He went in and grabbed his pouch of tobacco and made his prayers. "Wiyopeyata, wizopeyata, wiohianpata, itokagata," he whispered as he threw the double pinch of tobacco to Wakan Tanka. "Guide me, oh Grandfather," he whispered.

Bear was tired and lay down in his bed. It was four layers of buffalo robes that he curled up in. Toward the middle of the night he awoke and felt his medicine bag burning against his chest. He had made his decision. He would fight for the Blue Coats against slavery.

VI

In three days Bear stood facing Captain Morgan with a determined look on his face.

"I come to fight," said Bear.

The Captain beamed with delight. "God, that's good. I know you are a warrior to be proud of." Captain Morgan pulled out a Bible, then thought about it. "Are you a Christian?" he asked.

"I follow Wakan Tanka," replied Bear.

"That's good. Now put your hand on your heart."

Bear did so, as he wondered at this ceremony for battle.

"Do you swear by Wakan Tanka to fight loyally for the Union army?"

"Yes," answered Bear.

"Welcome to this man's army," said the Captain.

Bear slept apart from the others and was given a blue shirt to wear. He looked at it with curiosity.

"That's so one of our guys doesn't shoot you by mistake," said the crusty sergeant. "We're an informal group of raiders, lots of confusion when the bullets start flyin'. You already got a fine horse," he said. "Let's find out if'n you can shoot."

Bear let a cool smile wander over his face. "Good enough," he said.

"Well," said the sergeant. "You gotta show me." He was exasperated at Bear's cool manner.

Bear looked around. He saw some pots hanging from a line. "Last pot," he said. He drew both his 36s and put six shots into the pot, knocking it off the line. The men came out of their tents, weapons in hand, wondering if they were being attacked.

One man ran to get the pot. "Goddamn!" was all he said. It appeared to have six holes drilled in the bottom.

"Well, I guess that settles that," said the sergeant. "He can shoot."

Before long Captain Morgan came walking around Bear's tent with an armload of clothes and boots.

"You're a big man," he said to Bear. "Hard to find uniforms big enough to fit you."

Bear flinched at that. He would rather dress like a warrior.

"It's for your own safety," said Morgan, seeing Bear's dislike for the White man's clothes. "If you wear these then some yahoo like Bailey here won't shoot you out of hand just 'cause you're an Indian. Surely you see the sense in that."

Bear did see the sense in that and in the privacy of his tent quickly rummaged through the pile of clothes Morgan had brought him for a blue shirt and a pair of good boots. When he was dressed and stood tall he looked Union, but still every inch a Crow warrior.

"Captain," Bear said, "Must I listen to this horse-head of a sergeant about fighting?"

"For now," Morgan said. "But if you see him not doing the best tactics, you tell him. You are my eyes, Bear Itaxsca."

It seemed slow going, but soon the command had shifted to Bear. He had them whipped into the best Crow raiding party money could buy. They rode like a well-oiled machine. They rode to destroy Confederate held railroads and kept the larger enemy army harried and off balance.

Bear killed far more than he wanted to, but soon the message came to them about a major Confederate push to take the West.

"They're calling it The Battle of the Wilderness," Captain Morgan said. "Our job is to get all them Rebs that leak out and behind our lines."

Bear had become hard as stone in this White man's army. He disliked the war, it's noise and brutality and it was good that he was on the edges, not right in the middle.

The last day he spent hunting Rebs with Captain Morgan came. It was a cold and frosty morning; a dull low cloud covered the sky. It spoke of snow. Bear could feel the nip of cold on his face and hands and his guns seemed cold to the touch. That nervous, unsettled feeling was on everyone.

Men fumbled with the handles on their weapons and had the look of faraway eyes.

VII

The crash and fog of battle was all around Bear. He saw men in front of him dressed in Blue and Grey. All were in a desperate survival frame of mind; kill or be killed. The smoke and noise was intolerable.

A crazed face came out of the din and Bear shot it.

"Mother, oh, I'm damned. Mama," cried wounded dying men. Bear saw a walking Grey soldier, carrying his severed arm. The stink of blood was all around. He rode his horse to the top of a knoll. Then there was sudden silence.

All about him were the dead and dying. None seemed to have survived but him.

Then faintly from behind him came a weak cry. "Bear, Bear! We have won!" Bear turned to see a mortally wounded Captain Morgan, his back propped up against a rock. He was bleeding from several bullet wounds and coughing as he tried to breathe.

"We won, Bear." He looked longingly at the Crow warrior. His eyes glazed over, and he was dead.

The medicine bag about Bear's neck burned with a fury. It was time for him to leave this place. His company had all been killed in that last charge. It was time to go.

He picked the Captain's body up and laid it across a stray horse he found there.

He rode north until he found the Union Army camp. Reserves had already taken possession of the field of battle. They dug graves and planted the fallen.

He rode to the command tent, dismounted, and walked in the front of the tent, pulling aside the flap.

"Captain Morgan is here," he said. He could see all the soldiers reach for their guns, but then they realized he was also dressed in the Blue Union shirt and thought better of it.

"Poor bugger," said one of the corporals.

"Thank you for bringing him in," said a short gray-haired man. He was a colonel by his insignia.

"I am done with this," Bear said flatly. Too many horrific faces danced behind his tired eyes.

"That's alright, soldier," said the colonel. "We just got word that Lee surrendered three days ago, Back East. War's been over for three days and we just now got the word."

"What about Captain Morgan?" asked Bear.

"Oh, we'll get to him in a couple of days," said the colonel with a sheepish look on his face.

"I will see to him," said Bear. No one argued with him.

Bear took the Captain's body to the hill west of the encampment, a rocky area that over looked the valley.

"This is high enough for you Morgan," he said aloud. Bear dug a shallow grave and then built a cairn over the Captain's body. He piled the rocks about four-foot high over him, then he sang the Crow death song and wept. When he was done he put the Captain's hat on the grave and said good-bye.

The nearest town was Fort Smith. He was far south of the Crow lands, and the land seemed to be struck with a dearth. Nothing to hunt and nothing to eat. He had just enough supplies to get him to Fort Smith about a hundred miles to the east.

The war was done and everywhere he rode he could see the long nervous faces of people in disbelief. Away from the battlefield he passed overturned wagons and wounded men hobbling to some unknown destination.

No one spoke to him as he rode through the desolation. As he neared Fort Smith he ran into Union patrols, hungry men given the impossible task of reuniting a country, fearful that it would all start again.

"Hey there!" shouted one as Bear passed. "An injun in uniform. God damned, even they got into it."

Bear knew he stood out in the crowd of Whites and he didn't like it. The bitterness rose in his throat and he knew a hatred like his brother Joseph's for a time. But he had $25 in his pocket and needed provisions. He was headed back to the banks of the Shoshone River. He would be part of his people again.

He shook his head in realization. "No," he said aloud. "They will not take me back. They have turned their backs on me. I am alone."

"Hey you!" shouted a soldier. "What's your rank, where do you come from?"

It was the guard detail assigned to keep order in the town.

"Bear Itaxsca," he answered. "I am a scout for Phillip Morgan, western division.

"Why aren't you with your company?"

"I am all that is left of my company," answered Bear.

"You'd better come with me," said the private. "You guys are heroes. Some say you won the war single handed."

Bear was silent but followed the eager young soldier to a large hotel just outside the fort.

"Tie your horse up. The judge will be wanting to speak to you."

Bear secured Horse and walked slowly up the long staircase that could be seem through the large open doors. He felt like a prisoner going to his doom. The private followed him.

"Don't allow no guns," said the guard at the top of the stairs. "You'll have to leave 'em with me."

The one thing Bear had never been separated from was his guns.

"Then the judge can come out here and speak to me," Bear said.

He saw a chair and sat down. The guard went back into the larger room, presumably to tell the judge about Bear's refusal to give up his guns. There was a great deal of talking and then a man, about forty, burst out of the double doored hall.

"What's all this?" the judge growled. "You won't give up your guns?"

"Are you the judge who wants to see me?" asked Bear.

"Yes, I am," answered the other man. He was a tall grim looking man with close set eyes and a large nose. His piercing gaze gave one the feeling that he was always in charge.

His hands gripped the sides of his vest, the knuckles whitening with the pressure.

"Damn it!" he said. "I wanted to thank you for helping the Union! I've heard stories of your valiant effort for our country."

"I fought against slavery with my friend, Captain Morgan."

"Where is he?" asked the judge, his voice a bit calmer.

"He has passed on," said Bear. His grave is on that far hill." Bear pointed north west.

"He was a fine man, and a good soldier," said the judge. My name is William T. Crispen. And if you are not completely worn out, I have a job for you."

"What might that be?" asked Bear.

"Hunting," said Crispen.

"Hunting what?" asked Bear.

"Men!" said Judge Crispen. "You are just the sort I need to hunt down the criminals that plague my court!"

Bear smiled. "And what is my pay for all this?" he asked. He suspected nothing but a hard time.

"The bounties I set."

Bear had seen wanted posters before - $500 for so and so.

"I am a Crow," Bear said. "That is enough to be cheated throughout the White man's world!"

"No one will cheat you," said Crispin, because you will be my right arm. I will give you a number that guarantees the full force of the federal government behind it. Are you interested?"

"I do not hunt men," said Bear.

"Alright. Let's look at it another way," said Crispin. "You would be helping your people, the Crow."

Bear's eyebrows lifted with interest.

"The men I am talking about are criminals, some prey on the Native Americans with gall and hatred. I hear stories of them selling blankets carrying cholera or diphtheria to the Crow, sickness no medicine can cure. They use Crow women for prostitutes and slaves. Those are the men I want you to hunt."

Bear felt his medicine bag burn. Once again, he was being directed by his grandfather, the Itaxsca.

"I am your man," Bear said with certainty.

"Good. Good," said the judge.

Judge Crispin led Bear into the big room, with Bear's guns still at his waist. The judge reached into his desk and brought out a shiny new badge.

"You will be number 96994," he said. "You are now a federal bounty hunter. Within the confines of the United States of America none shall block you from pursuing criminals. Do you swear to it?"

"I swear to it," said Bear. He put the badge on his purple satin sash, next to his guns.

"Good. Good." Said Crispin. "Be my right arm."

VIII

"You can start in the territories," said Judge Crispin. "There is a man called Salisito that has preyed on Union supply trains. My other hunters have been unable to apprehend him. I have great hopes for you."

Bear rested for a day at the hotel. The sign said, 'No Indians,' but when he asked for a room he laid his Colt .44 on the desk in front of the clerk. "Yes sir," was all the man said as he handed the key to Bear.

Bear made sure the room number eleven was secure. He put a stick in the window and backed a chair under the door. He knew many Whites hated Natives and he was in no mood for a fight. Before he rested, he prayed. He took a pinch of tobacco and threw it to the four directions and Wakan Tanka and asked, "May this day go smoothly, and thank you for my life."

It was a good rest. It had been a long time since Bear had slept in a bed in relative security.

"So now I am to be the hunter of men," he said to himself, musing on the turn of his life's fortunes. He drifted off into a much needed sleep.

In the morning Bear awoke to gunfire in the plaza. When he looked out the window he could see a gathering crowd. They gathered to watch the execution of Rebel spies. Even though the war was over, these men had been judged and sentenced. He shook his head. The White man was a cruel and unjust creature. He felt the deep loss of life.

A knock came on his door.

"Yes," he called out.

"Judge Crispin wants to see you," said the voice.

"I will be there in a little while," Bear answered.

He threw on his boots, pants and guns, and ran a comb through his hair. He had cut it short so that it wouldn't get in the way during battle. Now he was bound to let it grow long again.

Bear went downstairs, snatched a cup of coffee from the bar and proceeded across the street to the great hall. There in the foyer sat William T. Crispin with an anxious look on his face.

"Bear," he said. "I have new information about the man Salisito."

"Yes?" questioned Bear.

"He has taken to robbing trains out West," said Crispin. "I am going to put you on a train that I know he will want to rob."

"You want me to welcome him to surrender?" asked Bear.

"He is wanted Dead or Alive," said Crispin. "Use your own judgment."

Later on that day Bear found himself at the railhead putting Horse in the car that carried the animals. Horse had a car all to himself with hay and oats to eat. Bear was satisfied that he would be safe.

"I will be in the passenger car," he said to Horse. "We have criminals to catch."

The horse licked his lips and nuzzled Bear to let him know he was okay. Horse had been his companion and partner since he was nineteen. The bond between them was unbreakable.

Bear smoothed Horse's mane and shook his ear, then left him for the passenger car. His job was to wait until Juan Salisito made his move, then to arrest or kill him; it didn't matter which one. He had seen much death. He would rather take him in, but all in all, it worked out the same in the eyes of the law.

Bear seated himself in the back of the passenger car. It was uncomfortable sitting still, and he grew stiff before long.

The country rolled by flat at first, then they climbed into the Rockies. His ears popped with the elevation, and the engine struggled on the harder slopes; nothing much seemed to be happening.

Bear dreamed about the war and about the last fierce battle. It was his unit who routed the Rebs away from the lines. The Union soldiers rolled over them and joined the main cavalry. There were only three men left at the end of the day and Captain Morgan took a mini ball in the upper chest. Morgan could barely struggle to the ground, bleeding profusely. In the dream Bear knew the captain wouldn't make it, but he tried to stop the bleeding.

Again in the dream, the Captain whispered, "We won, we won!" then his eyes glazed over; he took one last breath and was dead.

There was a jolt and Bear was shaken awake. His hands went to his guns. He soon came to his senses. He was sweaty and his heart was beating fast, coming so abruptly out of the dream world he was in. He looked around and noticed the train was climbing higher into the mountains. He could hear the labored chug of the engine as it pulled the steep grade.

He wondered again "When will Salisito make his play? This sitting and waiting is getting on my nerves."

Suddenly there was an explosion to the left which sent a hail of stones and debris down in front of the engine and onto the tracks. The train ground to a stop with a terrible thud and lurch at the end. "Salisito!" yelled one of the passengers.

Bear got up to investigate and noticed six men on horseback gathering around the engine. One had a flat brimmed Spanish hat. They had the engineer down on his knees, a gun to his head.

Bear calmly went to the exit and jumped out onto the berm next to the tracks. He approached the six men from the high ground the berm offered.

"Is this a party?" he asked. "Can anyone join in?"

They saw his badge gleaming in the sun and pulled their guns.

Bear dropped the first one with his right hand .36. He felt a bullet whiz past his ear, sounding like an angry bee. The second and the third fell just the same.

"Put 'em up," he yelled. "I'm looking for Salisito!"

The man with the flat Spanish hat stepped out of the gun smoke. He looked hard at Bear.

"You got him senor." The man said. "What is it you want?"

"I am a federal bounty hunter," Bear replied. "There's paper on you."

"You talk big for a man who is all alone," said Salisito. "How do you propose to collect that bounty?"

Bear saw that he was a man that would call his bluff. Salisito looked self-assured that he could handle any law-man.

"You've shot three of my men," said Salisito. "Do you think I can just let you walk away?"

Bear saw him move; Salisitos' right hand drew a gun. Bear shot, and in the slow motion of the act, he saw a red hole grow just below Salisitos' left cheek bone.

Salisitos' bullet grazed Bear's left ear lobe. Both men dropped to the ground with a thud. Bear could feel the trickle of blood on his shoulder; Salisito was beyond feeling anything.

The other two men beat a hasty retreat, leaving Bear four dead men to transport and three horses.

"That was fine shooting," said the old engineer. "You just got Juan Salisito. They been after him since the war began."

Bear went over to Juan Salisitos' body, took the flat brimmed Spanish hat from his head and carefully put it on his own.

"You were valiant," Bear said quietly to the dead man. I will remember you."

Soon the tracks were cleared. All the passengers lent a hand at moving the rocks from the blast. Bear loaded the bodies into the baggage car. The next stop was Carson City. He would collect his bounty there.

The Carson City sheriff met the train at the depot. He came into the passenger car noisily.

"Where is the devil that got Salisito?" he said playfully.

"It was me," said Bear.

"But you're an Injun!" the sheriff said in surprise.

"I am Officer 96994," Bear said. He looked at the sheriff with distaste.

As Bear stood up the sheriff eyed him with suspicion. He looked Bear up and down, and catching the gleam of Bear's badge, just shook his head.

"Well, come along to the office," the sheriff said. "We got paper work to do."

Bear could see the prejudice in the sheriff's eyes and that cold unwanted feeling swept across Bear like cold water.

"Do you read?" asked the sheriff.

"Fluently," said Bear.

"Well, you hit the jackpot this time Injun," the sheriff said. "Government is paying $1,200 for ole Salisito, and $500 for Flat Nose Mike."

"Let's go on over to the bank and see about getting your money."

The banker was a snooty fellow, the type with rimless glasses and a look on his face as if he were handling something dirty as he faced Bear.

"Ahh, yes," he said. "You know in this state Indians aren't allowed to have more than $500 per month?"

"That does not apply to me," said Bear. "I am a federal officer. My race has nothing to do with it."

"I'll have to get confirmation," said the banker. It took three hours, but finally a telegraph message came back with two words on it.

"Pay him," from William T. Crispin, Federal Judge.

"I can open up an account for you, Mr. Itaxsca," the banker said with a raised eyebrow.

"Cash will do just nicely," said Bear. "Gold if you can, it spends better. Bear had already seen the phony script backed by such and such a bank that no longer existed; the paper money was worthless.

In the end Bear walked out with two saddle bags filled with gold coin equaling $1,700. It was enough to buy a ranch.

Bear went over to the Silver Dollar Saloon and Hotel. He struck quite an oddity to the citizens of Carson City, Nevada. He was a six foot, one inch Crow warrior with a flat brimmed Spanish hat, two Colt 36s and a Navy 44, stuck in a purple silk sash. He wore Army pants and shirt, blue with a yellow leg stripe and heavy Army boots. People scurried to step aside when he walked.

Horse was stabled at a place called Guttermans. The man's eyes popped when Bear laid two twenty dollar gold pieces in his hand and said, "The best for my pony."

"Yes, sir, Mr. Injun" the stable man said. "Yes, sir."

He wondered if the man knew his business, but at this point he was exhausted. He needed sleep.

He walked into the Silver Dollar Hotel and stepped up to the check-in desk. Bear drew his .44, cocked it, and laid it on the desk.

"Room 11 if you have it," he said.

The clerk didn't say a word. He just reached back and snagged the keys. "You can make your mark if you will on the register," the clerk said politely.

Bear signed it 'Bear Itaxsca.'

He picked up the keys and went upstairs to room 11. It was a good room, a nice soft bed and two windows. The room had a chest of drawers with a china bowl and ewer full of water to wash in and a toilet. Bear smiled at the notion of indoor plumbing, a fascinating concept.

Bear was under no illusion. He had close to $1,700 in gold on him and he was a Native, which meant that he had no rights under the law. The possibility of his being robbed was an ever present danger. He would leave for San Francisco in the morning, he thought, and find a reputable bank. But right now – he did his ritual; he found two sticks to block the windows from opening and put a chair backwards under the doorknob. He also slept with his guns beside him. It would be a long and dreamless sleep.

The Grandfather

The Silver Ring

Bear awoke with a jolt from the dream he was having. Guns, smoke, and the agonized cry of wounded and dying men. The war had taken its toll on Bear Itaxsca and it had left scars that would never be erased. Beside him slept Helen. She was beautiful and the best lover he had ever had. He did not know about being in love with her, but it was the closest he had ever come to that elusive emotion. He knew something was pulling him though to find his people. Wakan Win said they were beyond Eagle Mountain, to the north. He was well off, he thought, over ten thousand dollars in the Whiteman's bank. Blood money it was true, but it spent just the same.

"You are magnificent," muttered Helen as she stretched naked in the bed beside him. She reached over and touched him gently. "Watcha thinking?"

Bear smiled at her. "It's been a long time away from my people," he answered. "I need to find them and reacquaint myself with the tribe."

"So, you are going to run off and leave?" she asked.

"Being here with you is good," he replied. "But there is a hole here where my heart is. It needs to be filled again. I have been away too long."

"Where does your tribe live?" she asked.

"The Wakan Win said they are beyond Eagle Mountain, north of the Shoshone River," he answered. "They are in trouble I think."

"Well," Helen said. "And I am here in Durango, and you've got a home and bed here any time you want it."

"Why?" he asked.

"You saved me and my kids," she said. "And, you gave me enough to buy that saloon. It all came from you. And..." she paused as she chewed her words. "You are the best lover I've ever had." A little girlish giggle escaped her lips.

"Helen is beautiful," Bear said to her softly. She was tall for a woman, well breasted with a tight stomach. Gentle on the eyes, with graceful hands. It didn't seem he had ever seen a woman as beautiful as her.

Just then a knock came at the door and the voice of a man called out. "Mr. Itaxsca," he said. "There's a wire message for you at the telegraph office. They sent me over to tell you."

"Thank you," said Bear. Helen noticed he had grabbed one of his guns as he spoke.

"You gonna shoot me with that?" asked Helen playfully.

"Old habits die hard," Bear said.

After Bear had dressed and had a cup of coffee, he made his way to the telegraph office. People shied away from him, looking down as he passed. He made a rather imposing figure, with the Wolf Collared coat, Spanish hat and all those weapons. The clerk at the telegraph office looked up as he approached.

"Mr. Itaxsca?" he asked.

"Yes," Bear replied.

"Message for you from Fort Smith."

'It had to be Crispin,' Bear thought. 'But how'd he know I was in Durango?'

"Thank you," said Bear. He reached out and took the paper from the clerk. It read: "Good work with Apache Joe. Someone else to hunt. Ex-Confederates selling diseased blankets to the Indians. Find them. Put a stop to it." - Crispin.

That was serious business Bear thought. He would have to find his tribe and work back from there. It was a big country; the Confederates could be anywhere.

He went back to the saloon and Helen was busy tending bar. He looked down and there was Dog, waiting for him with that sardonic expression on his face. Dog just cocked his head and lifted his ears. He knew they would be off soon.

"Well, I got word from Crispin," Bear said to Helen.

"Wants me to find some ex-Confederates selling blankets full of sickness to the Crow."

"You're going again," she said. "Just when I got my hands on you."

"Don't know where I'm going yet," said Bear. "Gotta ask around and see what the word is."

"Well, you might start with old Tanka Te," said Helen. "He grooms horses over at the livery. He seems to know everything about the Natives around here."

"That's a good idea," said Bear. "Think I'll mosey over and talk to him."

Bear ordered a solid breakfast- a slab of Ham and four eggs with chopped up country potatoes. He offered a generous piece of the ham to Dog who smacked his lips in appreciation. Then Bear and Dog went down the street to the livery.

The ground was wet and muddy. His boots squished in the tracks of wagons and hooves. There had been a light snow in the night, early some said – a tracker's snow that let all the prints stand out.

"Cha da cho," Bear said to the old man brushing down the horse in front of him.

The old man, a thousand wrinkles in his leathered face, had expressionless eyes. He looked around the mount curiously.

"Cha da cho, Itaxsca," he croaked in return. He was short for a Crow, dressed in a flannel shirt and dirty jeans. He seemed to know Bear, but Bear had no recollection of him.

"You are Tanka Te?" asked Bear.

"The very same," he said with a wink. "What does the grandson of Itaxsca want of me?"

"I was told you knew a lot," Bear answered. "I come for wisdom from you if I can."

"I work for the Whites," said Tanka Te. "I have no wisdom to give." He seemed a little bitter edged.

"I would like to know some far off gossip about our tribe," said Bear.

Takan Te's eyes seemed to brighten. "Shall we smoke?" he said.

"That would be a pleasure," replied Bear.

"The back of the barn is good," said Takan Te.

The old man put his brush down, patted the horse he'd been brushing down, and went over to a cupboard and took out a long leather bag.

"Follow me," he said. They went around to the back of the barn. There was some scattered hay there and a small fire pit. "Make me a fire," said the old man to Bear. Bear got to work and soon had dragged up some brush wood and had a small blaze going.

Takan Te removed his pipe from the leather bag. It was a plain wooden and stone carved thing, and he started tamping an herb into the bowl. "Let us sit," he said. They had two wooden boxes from the barn for chairs. The sun was warmer there away from the breeze.

Takan Te offered bits of tobacco to the four winds, just as Bear did every day. Then he said to Bear in a commanding voice, "Light me."

Bear pulled a burning branch from the fire and lit Takan Te's pipe. As the old man offered him the pipe, Bear touched the pipe stem to his left shoulder, then his right, sharing the pipe ceremony with Takan Te.

Finally, the old man looked at Bear and said, "You want to know about Samson, the trader."

Bear was puzzled. "Who is he?"

"Oh, he be that guy who sells rifles without firing pins, blankets full of sickness in them for a high price to the People. The tribe has had its fill of the Whiteman's diseases. Many have died," he continued. "Time someone put an end to him."

"Do you know where his territory is?" Bear responded.

"Well, that's the trouble," Takan Te said. "He's like a ghost. Shows up, then disappears."

Bear could see he had a job catching up to him.

"Can you just point me in a direction?" asked Bear.

"Go north and east past Eagle Mountain, is what I heard," Takan Te said. "Up by your tribe on the Shoshone River."

Now the medicine bag Bear wore around his neck began to burn slightly. That's where he would hunt for this man. Home on familiar territory.

Bear left a pouch of tobacco for Takan Te on the work bench. He knew the gift had to be in secret, a thank you for the information. Inside the pouch he left a twenty-dollar gold piece.

Takan Te had gone back to currying the horses. He paid Bear Itaxsca no more mind as if he had no connection to him.

Bear walked back to the saloon, past the little houses and store fronts that all looked old and rickety to his eyes. It seemed a good strong wind could blow them into history, but there they stood, frowning at him.

He was up the steps and into the saloon, Dog right at his heels. Helen was behind the bar, now washing glasses. She looked at him and said, "Get what you need?"

"I'll be leaving in the morning." Bear had learned not to say anything about his movements in public. Helen seemed to grow in wisdom. She just nodded her head.

"I have a question for you," she said.

"Shoot," Bear replied.

"What's in the bag you have hung from you neck?"

"It is medicine from my grandfather," he replied.

"Yeah, but what is it?" she asked.

"Don't know; I've never looked," he answered.

"Hmm," she remarked. "I wonder..."

Bear looked at her and added, "If I look it may be the magic might escape and then it would be worthless."

Helen reached over and tweaked his ear with her fingers. "I could see that," she said.

"I'll be off, North, tomorrow," he said. "There is a man named Samson that's selling those diseased blankets - contaminated blankets. I have to stop him."

"You wouldn't let me ride along, would you?" asked Helen.

Bear chuckled. "You would be good to have with me on the trail," he said. "But it is dangerous and might get us both killed. Sometimes it is very hard out there."

Helen nodded that she understood.

III

Bear woke the next morning before dawn. Helen was warm beside him. She stretched with eyes still closed, crossing her legs ever so delicately at her ankles; she was a pleasure just to look at. Bear thought about taking up teepee living, letting everything go south. But the small ache in his head told him that business needed to be done. He slid out of bed and quietly pulled on his clothes. He had just put the last of his guns into his sash when Helen made a small moan.

"You're leaving, aren't you?" she whispered.

"Yes," he said. "but if I am able to return, I will be here with you."

"That's good to know," she said.

Bear went downstairs and found the cook who had been in the kitchen for hours. The cook obliged Bear with a plate of steaming food.

"Ya'll better eat 'fore you go off wanderin'," he said. His name was Henry. He was an old freed slave, a Southern man.

"Come have a taste with me," Bear invited.

Henry cut off a chunk of steak for himself and popped it in his mouth.

"Mm," he said. "I will sit with you. I understand Mr. Bear, and I thank you for sitting with me," he said. "The war's over, but there's still a lot of hatred."

"I'm still alive because I'm careful," said Bear. "Indians have to be."

Henry just nodded. They both knew their place.

One last cup of coffee, then Bear headed for the livery where Horse was stabled. He walked in and there Horse was, saddled and ready to go. Takan Te stood looking at Bear. "Good horse," he said. "Keep him safe."

"Thank you," Bear remarked, surprised that his elder knew he was leaving at this hour.

"Try not to blow your foot off with that damned beef rifle of yours," Takan Te said sardonically as he turned and walked away. "Hetche tuelo, let it be so" Takan Te said in blessing.

"Hetche tuelo" Bear answered him.

IV

Bear was feeling restless. His medicine bag had burned against his chest all night long and Dog was restless. They both knew a fight was coming; they just didn't know from whom or where. He rode Horse gently and kept a sharp eye on the trail ahead. His guns were clean and freshly loaded; his knife was razor sharp. He was ready. Ahead on the trail he saw an Indian warrior. Bear raised his hand in greeting, but there was no response from the Native man. The warrior's eyes were intense and then they flashed. There was a roll of thunder and the man was gone. A spirit giving warning.

The medicine bag burned again. Bear knew it was a premonition. 'What's going on?' he wondered.

Soon, as he approached a rocky cutting in the trail, he saw three braves with blankets wrapped around them as they stood shivering in the morning light. Their fire had burned low and as Bear approached he could see the illness that was upon them.

"Cho da cha," he said from a distance.

"Cho da cha," one replied. We are sick with the fever," said the one in the middle. "You'd better ride on."

"Did you trade for blankets with a man named Samson?" Bear asked.

The one brave just looked hard at him.

"If you did," Bear said "They have a sickness in them. Burn them and you will begin to feel better."

"Who are you that tells us this?" asked the one in the middle.

"I am Bear Itaxsca," he said.

"The Itaxsca is dead. Who are you really?" the man asked angrily.

"I am his grandson," Bear said. Bear could see they did not believe him. He reined Horse in and continued up the trail. As he looked back there was a larger fire blazing up. They trusted him enough and were burning the blankets.

It was the beginning of September and Bear felt a frost in the air. He would have to winter camp from now on, especially in the higher elevations. The trail up to the Yellowstone was rocky, and if it snowed before he reached there, it would be impassable. Still it was nearer to his country. He felt a strange sense of being part of the land, as if it was welcoming him home.

Bear was six days out of Durango when he first came on the traders. These were men heavily armed, with wagons full of goods for anyone who would buy them. Mostly they were solitary sorts, just trying to make a living after the war. Some though, had the stink of evil about them. One of those Bear came upon three days out from the Yellowstone. The man was a dreadful pock-marked man, with narrow eyes and a hunched shoulder. He carried a Henry 45-70 lever action in his lap.

"Cha da cho!" Bear yelled at him. "Where do you go?"

The man caught sight of Bear's badge and reined in his horses.

"Ain't goin' nowhere," he said. "Just up country to sell to settlers."

"What you got there?" asked Bear.

"Oh, blankets, and flour, some rice and dry bean. You know, just staples and such."

"I'm looking for a trader named Samson," Bear said. "You know such a man?"

"Don't recollect," said the shifty eyed trader.

"Well, there's a price on his head," said Bear directly. "He's been trading blankets with sickness in them to the Crow Indians."

The trader became nervous and feigned friendliness. "Damn, that's bad for business," he said.

"It's cold," Bear said. "Why don't you wrap yourself in one of those blankets you got. You'd be a lot warmer."

"I'm good," he said.

"No!" Bear insisted. "I see you got some of those diseased blankets. Military issue it looks like. You got them from Samson, didn't you?" Bear barked.

"What if I did?" The man whined back at him.

"Then you gotta dump your load right here and burn it," Bear commanded. "I ain't lettin' you trade that to my People."

"Please, Mister," he whined again. "Let me do my work. If I let this load go Samson will nail my hide to a barn door."

"Unhitch the team," ordered Bear. Dog gave a long low growl.

The man made a sudden move. The barrel of his rifle came up and a shot rang out. It grazed Bear's right cheek like a stinging bee flying at the speed of sound. But before the man could fire another, Bear had drawn his 36 from the sash and shot the trader just below his left ear into his jawline. The man gasped, his eyes staring in surprise, and then he slumped over in the wagon seat.

Bear took out his knife and cut the reins of the horses and shot into the air to make them scatter. He saw a barrel of powder in the wagon. He rode off one hundred paces and took his rifle out. One precise shot and the barrel ignited, blowing up the wagon and the corpse of the dead trader. It burned with the fury of hell.

Bear waited until the fire had consumed everything, and he silently turned Horse north again.

Bear knew that Native medicine could not cure this epidemic of disease. Small pox had almost run the land clean of Natives when the Spanish came in the 1500s. This was worse; fire was the only remedy to purify a stricken village. His anger at the Samson trader became real and intense. He would find and kill this man.

Bear came to the crossroads. West was the Denver trail, east was into the plains. He figured the high plains country trail would lead to the wagons and traders that worked for the Samson. He knew of a small town nestled on the trail about sixty miles north of him that was in the direction of the Yellowstone. He pointed Horse in that direction and rode onward. He was in no hurry. He wanted to take in the whole country and he knew he was in Arapaho hunting grounds. They were fearsome enemies, especially for a lone Crow warrior.

It was cold, and he chose a place just off the trail to make camp. The steel gray sky was turning red as the sun set. 'The Great Rockies are swallowing the sun,' he thought as he laughed to himself. That's what his Grandfather, the Itaxsca, used to say. Bear thought of his family, the tribe, and the life that he had walked away from to fight against slavery. Except for knowing his friend, Captain Morgan, it had been a fool's errand. 'There will always be slaves,' Bear thought. 'I can do more to fight slavery as I am now, hunting down slave owners.'

The sun had gone down and the chill blew against him. Horse and Dog kept close to the fire as did Bear. Dog nestled into Bear's belly, getting warm and napping.

Suddenly there was a noise. Into the firelight crept a small red fox.

"Your camp is cold," said a voice from the shadows.

"Not for you," Bear said. He recognized the ancient quavering voice of Wakan Win. "Come into the light. There is food."

Into the light of the fire where Bear was sitting, struggled the old Woman.

"You choose to visit me at strange times," said Bear.

"It is only when I am needed." She said. They sat in silence while she chewed on a bit of jerky he offered, and she drank a cup of pejuta sapa, the black medicine, camp coffee.

"It does get cold this time of year," she said. "How is my boy getting along?"

He smiled. This time she seemed to be the spirit of his mother looking in on him.

"You said there is danger?" he questioned.

"Your grandfather sends a message," she said. "Don't forget the silver ring."

"What silver ring?" asked Bear.

She looked at him as though he was a child and said "tisk, tisk," at him. "The one you wear about your neck," she said. "It is in your medicine bag, of course."

"I have not looked in it," Bear said. "I believe it would be bad luck to open it."

Her wrinkled face looked askance at him. "When you find your enemy, he will be powerful beyond those guns you wear, she said. "You can call down the lightning from above if you wear the ring. Has it not burned you before this?"

Bear knew it had. He was embarrassed and felt sheepish before her gaze.

"Sleep boy," she said. "And don't forget, you will be joined by another, soon. She will help you. Do not turn her away."

Bear suddenly felt very drowsy, and the last thing he saw was Wakan Win hobbling out of the fire light, her small fox marking the edge of her skirt like a cat.

V

Bear shook himself awake and his hand gripped the handle of his colt .36. It was almost dawn and the east grew rosy red under a swift sunrise. There was the noise of a horse being ridden close at hand. Its hooves slipped on the muddy trail. Bear swept into battle mode as he moved quickly into the bushes at the far side of his camp.

The unknown horse stopped on the trail above him. Bear was curious. Dog hadn't growled. He looked up and saw Dog's tail wagging in delight.

"Bear!" yelled a familiar voice. "Bear Itaxsca, are you there?"

It was Helen. "Damn that woman!" he growled to himself. She had not stayed home.

"Come ahead," he said loudly.

Down the slippery bank scooted Helen Hardin. She was all smiles and glad to see Bear.

"I thought I told you not to come after me!" Bear said.

"Well," she paused. "I never was any good at taking orders," she said. "It struck me that if you went solo on this hunt I would never see you again. And Bear, I just couldn't do that. Emma and Charlie are safe with my sister, and you are my man. I 've decided that," she said. She sounded as if she had rehearsed that speech over and over, and she finally was able to say it aloud.

Bear felt like turning her over his knee and giving her a whack or two. She didn't know the danger she had put them both in.

"A woman is fair game out here," he said firmly. "And I don't even know if you can shoot or fight."

"I'm not much at fighting," she said. "But I can shoot."

"Show me," said Bear stubbornly.

She pulled aside her coat and there was a belt and holster slung from her hip with a colt.36 dangling at her side.

"Show me," he said again in disbelief.

"Hmm," she pondered. "That tree over there – about fifty yards away. The one above the sky line." She drew smoothly, fanned the hammer, and blew the top of the tree off. In one swift move she had reholstered the gun.

Bear didn't say a word. He frowned. He had asked, and she had shown him. Wakan Win was always right and this was the woman she had told him would come to help him.

"O.K." he said. "But you do what I tell you, when I tell you, and we might get out of this alive."

Helen smiled and said nothing.

"I plan on getting us up to Forsythe Camp. That's the last mountain settlement before the Yellowstone Trail. We will see what we will see there."

"I passed some of your work on the way," she said. "It was still smoldering ashes."

Bear swung into the saddle and pointed Horse's nose north. He hoped Wakan Win was right. 'Well,' he said to himself, 'she has learned to shoot.'

In three days they came down from the high trail to the small settlement of Forsythe. It wasn't a town yet, some broken down shacks and a lot of military style bivouac tents. The only permanent buildings were the saloon, a barn, and a whorehouse. Bear noticed some men hard at work building what looked to be a church.

"Where to now?" asked Helen.

"We look around," said Bear. "We look for news about the Samson and his men."

He tied Horse in front of the saloon and walked in like he owned it.

"We don't allow no Injuns in here," said the bartender.

Same old story – until Bear flashed his badge and laid his cocked .44 on the bar.

"You Federal?" The bartender asked.

"Yeah," said Bear. "Do you have any rooms here?"

"Upstairs," The bartender looked at Bear hard.

Bear returned the gaze. Helen and Dog came in and the bartender's eyebrows went up. "We don't allow any of that in here," he shouted.

Helen sidled over to the bar and tweaked the man's ear. "I'm the owner of the Silver Dollar Saloon down in Durango," she said. "And this is my man."

"O.K. ma'am," he said. "Take your Federal Injun up to room 9."

"Don't you have a room 11?" asked Bear.

"Naw," the bartender replied. "We only got ten rooms."

"That'll be fine," said Helen, as she laid twenty-dollar gold pieces on the bar in front of the man. Again, his eyebrows went up and he didn't hesitate to scoop them up and into his vest pocket. He handed Helen the key.

Under his breath Bear muttered, "Those damned Whites, think they own the world."

"I got the horses stabled," said Helen, trying to sound like his assistant. "Now what?"

"We lock ourselves in the room and sleep," said Bear.

Helen watched as Bear put a chair under the door knob, and two sticks in the windows. He hung his guns from the bed post, and one under his pillow, loaded and ready.

"They just don't like uppity Natives like me," he said to her. "Better safe than sorry."

Helen pulled off her duster, then jeans and boots. She slid into bed. "It's been a while," she said with a smile.

Bear smiled too. "That's what I meant by dangerous," he said. He had a woman that was his and she wouldn't let go. It was too easy for him to be distracted.

VI

The first daylight of morning peeked through the window of the room. Bear and Helen shared the bed, and Dog lay quiet in the corner. It was good to feel Helen pressed close to him.

This would be a hard fight and he hoped she had the muscle for it. Wakan Win told him not to turn her away. He was glad she was here.

"What next?" she whispered to him. She stretched, and Bear watched her beauty lying beside him.

"We go and visit the Natives that live on the edge of town," he said. "They are Flathead Indians and know a lot about what goes on here. They are not the same as Lakota or Arapaho."

Bear continued, "They might talk to me because they are afraid of Crow medicine."

"Doesn't it benefit them too?" asked Helen. "If we catch this Samson character?"

"Yes, but they live by what they trade," he answered. "They do not understand about sickness. They cannot see it and they do not want to cut off one hand just to help the Crow."

"Tribal rivalry," said Bear, responding to Helen's look of curiosity.

After they had dressed, Helen in her duster and old hat, Bear in his Spanish hat and Wolf collared coat, they went down stairs to see if they could get some breakfast.

"You must be ready to pop," he said to Dog. Dog just looked at him and then ran off. He would find them again after he had taken care of his own morning business.

"Is there any such thing as food around here?" Bear asked the bartender. The bartender just pointed outside to a tent across the street and said, "Molly's."

"Be careful," Bear said to Helen. "A White woman with a Native man is a sin to some folks. They may be looking for trouble."

"Yes," she said. "I can see this." Her eyes narrowed with resolve. "But they ain't gonna prevent us from eating."

She walked ahead of Bear and took a seat at Molly's. "Ham and eggs?" She asked the waitress. "Two plates please."

"Yes, Ma'am," said the girl as she took the order. The girl was very short and seemed harried. She was barefoot and had a runny nose. "Right away Ma'am." She said.

Bear joined Helen; all the eyes in the café were upon them.

When the two orders came, Helen took them both and laid one down in front of Bear. She played the part well, looking like she was feeding her Indian. Bear smiled.

The tension in the room lessened.

"Why don't they like Indians?" she asked.

"It goes back a long way," said Bear. "This is Flathead ceremonial ground. The Whites struck silver in the mountains and built a town of sorts right over that sacred land." Bear took a few bites of breakfast. "Then when the Flatheads fought to keep the sacred lands, the Whites damned near wiped them out. Both sides had aggravated each the other. I gotta tell you," he continued. "The Flathead don't like the Crow either. They are afraid of the tribe because they think the Crow are magic.

"Well, you are," said Helen as she tipped her head sideways and stared at him.

"Yeah," replied Bear. He kept his eyes down for a moment.

They finished breakfast and walked back to the livery to retrieve their horses. Helen caught a glimpse of the little waitress as they walked. She was on her knees in front of some miner, preparing to give him pleasure. She knew the direction that young soul would take.

Dog was waiting for them at the front doors of the livery and his tail wagged at their approach. Helen wondered how he kept himself fed, his coat always glossy and healthy.

"How do you keep him fed?" she asked Bear.

"He's a hunter." He replied. "Loves rats."

"This is a strange and wonderful relationship," mused Helen.

They saddled their horses and rode out to the edge of Forsythe. In the distance they could see the tops of some teepees. Smoke from the cooking fires drifted above the ragged line of trees that obscured the camp.

Helen rode several yards behind Bear. After hearing how unfriendly the Flathead were she didn't want to be leading this expedition.

"The chief's name is Bear Horn O'Doole," said Bear. "He is known to my tribe and is good for a tip about Samson. And, you've gotta act like you are my woman around them."

"You mean speak when I'm spoken to?" Helen replied.

"It's a different world you've put your foot in." Bear answered. "In this world, women, unless they are medicine women, or elders, are property."

"You mean...?" she blurted out.

"I mean it's a different world," Bear said. "I was your Injun back in town. Now you are my woman here."

With that realization Helen agreed. "O.K." and became quiet.

VII

They rode slowly toward the teepees and a few Natives stared at them with curiosity as they passed. Soon four Flathead hunters rode up and wanted to know why they had come into their village.

"Cha da cho," replied the lead warrior. He looked to be a man in his mid-twenties, strong and ready to defend his tribe from all comers.

"What do you want here, Crow?" he said evenly. He looked ready for a fight.

"I come from yonder," said Bear, pointing to the east. I would talk to your chief, Bear Horn."

"Do you have a name?" the warrior asked.

"Bear, Bear Itaxsca. I am known to your chief."

The other warriors were wide-eyed with fear and suspicion.

"You cannot be the Itaxsca," replied the warrior. "He is dead."

"I am his grandson," said Bear. "And I carry his medicine."

The warrior turned and thundered off to a large teepee at the edge of the camp. He dismounted, pulled back the teepee flap and entered. Soon he emerged again and vaulted onto his horse's back and came back to Bear.

"Bear Horn will see you," he said in a clipped tone. "You are to bring your woman too."

Helen played the part and looked down, then followed Bear at a slow walk. Dog kept his distance and stayed at the edge of the camp.

Bear was escorted into the teepee, and when his eyes grew accustomed to the dimness inside, he saw Bear Horn sitting, looking as regal as any king. His hair was in three great braids, oiled and shining in the light of a small fire. Two feathers stuck straight up from the back of the chief's head. His eyes seemed coal black in the dim light.

"Cha da cho, Itaxsca." He said.

"Hau," said Bear. "Why do you come this way?" Bear Horn inquired.

"To smoke with you," said Bear. "And to talk of small things."

"Hmm," replied Bear Horn, nodding his head.

Bear Horn snapped his fingers, and his pipe was brought to him carefully by an elderly woman. He slowly filled the pipe and lit it and handed it to Bear. Bear put the stem to his shoulder, then to his lips and drew smoke from it. He handed it back to Bear Horn.

"I am sorry to hear about your grandfather's passing," he said. "He was a great man. And I remember you. You were only twelve or thirteen when I saw you last."

"Time has passed," said Bear. "You were a friend to my grandfather."

"Yes," replied Bear Horn. "He helped in driving the plague away from our village. He was mighty in medicine for a Crow. What would you ask of me now?"

"I search for the trader called Samson."

"Not in peace I see," said Bear Horn.

"No," replied Bear slowly.

"The one you ask for is known to me," said Bear Horn. "He is not one to approach easily."

"I know nothing except that he is wanted for murder," said Bear. "He must be brought to justice."

"I see you carry the White man's badge of authority," Chief Bear Horn said. "How came you by it?"

"I fought in the great war against slavery," Bear said directly. "It is my pledge of duty."

"To the Whites?" chuckled Bear Horn. "They are false and will turn it on you. Even so, the man you seek has a house on the Yellowstone trail. Maybe sixty miles north of here, but I warn you, he has big medicine. You will not easily take him. Since the buffalo have gone, I trade for cattle to feed my people. Samson has a grudge against the Crow and would wipe the land clean of them; poison food, poison blankets, things the proud warriors cannot fight."

"I think I will go visit this Samson," said Bear. "We will come to terms."

"That is a fine woman you have there," Bear Horn said, changing the subject. "Would you trade for her?"

"No great chief," smiled Bear. "She is mine."

"Too bad," Bear Horn said. "Mine are all sour." They fell silent for a long moment.

Bear completed the amenities due to a chief of Bear Horn's stature and thanked him for his hospitality.

As Helen and Bear climbed into the saddle, she asked Bear, "What did he want with me?"

"He wanted to know if you were for sale."

Helen was indignant. "Well I never..." she started.

Bear interrupted. "You have stepped into this world. It isn't the same as in town.

Helen thought a while then said, "I'll keep that in mind."

VIII

The trail seemed long and lonely. Bear was busy looking ahead and behind. He felt that there was something or someone in the last few miles watching them. They had left the Flathead chief days ago and were now in country he was familiar with, Crow country, but it did not feel the same as he remembered.   All around him he felt a suspicious watchfulness. It was silent like an oncoming storm and was imminent. No birds sang. No deer sprang from the trail. It was quiet and ominous.

"What a creepy place," said Helen. "Does your tribe live here?"

Suddenly an arrow, seemingly shot from nowhere, stuck in the ground before him. Into view rode four Crow warriors.

"Don't talk unless you're spoken to," Bear warned aside to Helen.

"I see you!" Bear called out.

The one warrior rode ahead of the others toward him.

"You are Bear," he stated. "Why do you come back to your land?"

"I hear the groans under a bad magic." Bear replied.

"Come then, but beware," said the warrior. "The White man's sickness is all around. Many die."

Bear could feel his medicine bag flair into heat and burn his chest.

"And my father, Blue Knife?"

"They are beyond Eagle Mountain," said the warrior. "Up the Shoshone River."

"You are Four Ponies. I remember you when we were young," said Bear.

He and Helen rode down trail for most of the day until Bear could see the smoke from the village fires. As they neared the teepees he could hear the hacking and coughing of sick people. Only a few remained well enough to hunt.

"Ossiaro is chief," said Four Ponies.

Bear had a sudden urge to gather all the blankets and clothes and burn them.

"Itaxsca!" he heard from behind him.

"Bacheeitche. [*Chief*]" Bear called. "Ossiaro." Bear turned and rode toward the chief.

"We die." The chief said sadly. "Only the ring could save us now and the Itaxsca is dead. Do you have it?"

"I have it," said Bear quietly.

Without a thought he pulled open his medicine bag. There was the silver ring with a broad fire opal at the center. Bear put it on and lifted his hand to the sky. Spontaneously the wind blew, and lightning cracked from the clouds. A blue haze encircled the village. Fire burned all the disease into ash. It lifted men and horses into the air, crumbled teepees and all the land around seemed to groan as if a great weight had been lifted from it.

Then it was still. Those who had seemed near to death rose up and shook themselves, feeling suddenly well again. The blue fire had turned all the diseased clothes and blankets into dust. And Bear, his chest heaving with a rapidly beating heart, was on his knees staring at the silver ring upon his finger.

Ossiaro, old and shaking, approached him. He laid a hand on Bear's shoulder.

"The evil is gone, grandson of the Itaxsca."

"I know not what was done," said Bear. Fear was in his brown eyes. He was in disbelief at what had happened.

"Your grandfather did the same when the plague came in the year of the Otter, too many moons ago to count. The ring was all powerful and has proved itself so again."

"I've never..." Bear stammered. "I've never believed in the legends. Grandfather left me the medicine bag when he died. He never told me anything.

Ossiaro smiled. His wrinkled face and black eyes beamed with satisfaction. "The magic is not for all to wield. Only those who are worthy. Bear Itaxsca, you are worthy."

Bear quickly took the ring off and put it back in the medicine bag. He looked around at the village people whose eyes had grown large with amazement.

Helen approached him cautiously and asked, "Are you all right?"

"Yes," answered Bear, but his hands were still shaking. He tried desperately to get control of himself. Slowly he began to understand that he was the heir to the powerful talisman that his grandfather had given him. He needed to think and digest what had happened.

"We will camp a small way down the trail," he said to Helen. "Let us leave and when all is put back in order I will ask that Four Ponies come to get me. We need to smoke the pipe with the chief and talk about the Samson."

IX

Bear, Helen, Horse and Dog went up trail about two miles where they found a small hollow for a sheltered place to camp. It looked like it had been used for camp before. The hollow dipped down below the road into a knot of trees with a smooth grassy spot in the center. Someone had built a stone fire pit at the bottom and a small stream gurgled only a dozen yards from the hollow. Bear was silent until he had the fire going. He muttered to himself, "I am not a shaman."

He looked at Helen and asked her to describe what she had seen at the village.

"Well," she said slowly. "You put the ring on your middle finger, and the whole village was encompassed with a light blue flame. Clothes and blankets and teepees seemed to crumble into dust. The whole area felt as spent as a squeezed lemon. Then it was gone, and here you are."

"I have heard stories of my Grandfather," Bear said. "He was a great healer and had the respect of all the tribes around. They would come, Flathead, Crow, Arapaho, even Lakota, to get his blessing for their newborn children. He offered his gift freely whenever he was asked. I do not have his wisdom, and yet this time it worked."

Helen wrinkled her brow and said thoughtfully, "I think the ring is like a hammer. It defends the wearer from danger, any danger."

Bear looked at her in silence. She was smart, this woman of his. "It could be," he said.

It was dark, the fire burned low and Bear stared at the flames, blue, red and yellow, as they slowly turned to coals. He could not wrap his mind around the magic of the ring. The others, Dog and Helen, were long since asleep and peaceful in dreams.

"You have your grandfather's touch," said a voice from the shadows. It was Wakan Win. She crept into the firelight followed by her familiar, the fox. Bear handed her a large piece of jerky for her to chew on.

"I am myself, Mother," he said. "I am not Grandfather."

"You are a brave man," she said. "You have helped your tribe."

"What have you come to say?" he asked.

"Tomorrow you will get news about the Samson," she said. "Beware, he is a man of great medicine."

"So I hear," replied Bear.

"Helen can help you; let her," Wakan Win said.

"She sure can shoot," he said.

"Be sure you take care of that medicine you wear. It is a thing that can easily be spent."

She arose and faded into the night. The last Bear saw was her shuffling figure followed by her fox, disappearing just out of the circle of firelight.

He fell asleep surrounded by the warmth of the fire and his blanket.

As the sun rose it framed the face of Helen, still sleeping in her hammock. Bear had awakened from a dreamless sleep just before dawn. He built up the fire and was frying bacon in his small flat pan. He always carried it just in case he had the chance to cook.

"Hey, Sleepy," he said softly to Helen. "We're burning daylight."

Helen shrugged and rolled out of her hammock. "That was a great dream," she said.

Bear looked at her and she smiled. "I ain't telling," she said.

A sound of hooves on the road above them interrupted her.

"Itaxsca!" called out a voice. Bear recognized it was Four Ponies.

"Down here!" Bear called back. The straight backed young warrior rode his horse down into the hollow.

"Ossiaro would speak to you."

"Hai, I'll be along directly," answered Bear. Four Ponies reined his horse around and disappeared back down the road.

"You go," said Helen. "When you return I will have breakfast for you."

Bear leaped onto Horse and rode off to the village. He didn't often ride Horse bare-backed, but this was a short ride and he was in a hurry. Horse did not seem to mind.

Bear pulled Horse up short just outside the village and walked in. Ossiaro was sitting in front of a fire waiting like a patient spider. When he saw Bear he rose and looked long at him with those deep brown eyes, eyes that bore no emotion and seemed the color of shiny coal.

"You have come," he said solemnly. "Let us talk of the Samson.

Several years ago, some bad medicine, I believe it came from a man, came from the south. The man built a home here a little east of the Shoshone Valley. Your father, Blue Knife, tried to fight it, get the man to leave, but the medicine was too strong. This man's medicine had a way of turning light to darkness and living into dying. Your father fled with most of your clan and went beyond Eagle Mountain. This strange man's face was fair, a White man, but his intent was dark and evil. To wipe out all Crow and take the land for himself was his goal. He brought in traders who came to the people with blankets, weapons, and food, all of which were tainted with disease.

A shadow fell on the land. He lives in a huge White man's house about forty miles east of the Shoshone Valley. He has many men with him now."

Bear thought silently for a moment. "I only need to know where he is, Father. Is he a spirit?"

"No, he is flesh and blood, but he has a way about him that sucks the life out of everyone and everything."

"I will put an end to it," said Bear. "He is not some great bacheeitche to bow before."

"If anyone can put an end to him, it is you," said Ossiaro.

"Thank you for your information," Bear said. "I will go with care."

Helen had found some quail eggs and fried them with the pork slabs for Bear. His belly was full. He hoped his edge would not go from him if he was fat from this woman's good cooking. Bear and Helen packed up and took to the trail later that day.

"We head up north toward the Yellowstone," he told her. "Then east to the Shoshone Valley."

"This is your tribal ground isn't it?" she asked.

"Yes, but I've been gone so long the wind and trees have forgotten me. I feel like a stranger now."

The mountains loomed high toward the west; the snow-covered peaks stood silent, like sentinels watching the earth turn beneath them. The pine forested foothills at the side of the mountains were still and dark. Now and then a frightened deer or small covey of quail would leap off the trail in front of them. The leaves of the aspens had already turned yellow, and the silence of fall was in the air.

The ground is even quiet, "Bear said. "There must be a great medicine that keeps it that way."

They traveled for two days, putting in close to the trail to camp; guns remained in their hands at night.

"I feel someone is tracking us," Bear said.

Helen nodded, "I feel it too."

They were still two days from the Yellowstone on a flat stretch, when a man in a wagon sat on the trail ahead. Bear and Helen approached with caution.

"Cho da cha," shouted out Bear.

The man raised his hand.

"This doesn't feel right," said Helen.

"Keep your eyes on the trees," said Bear aside to her. "There's trouble coming."

Sure enough, shots rang out from the tree line. Helen slid off her horse with rifle in hand. She shot three times, bang, bang, bang. It was a frenzy that lasted maybe thirty seconds, with both Bear and Helen shooting at the intruders. There were a dozen men lying dead on the trail.

Good shooting," Bear said.

Helen was crying.

"You were defending yourself," Bear said with a scowl.

"I know..." she replied. "I'm okay."

The man who had been on the trail had disappeared when the shooting started. Bear reckoned they had not seen the last of Samson's men.

All was quiet as they moved on. The wind seemed to suck itself out of the valley, and it became as still as death. Bear could hear the rustle of vulture wings circling the dead. The land had a sickness about it.

The noise of horse hooves rang loud on the ground.

"Jesus, it's creepy here," Helen said. "Even the river sounds muffled. It's not loud enough."

"It is some dark medicine," said Bear. "And it knows that we are here."

They road into the valley of the geysers. It was early morning and the darkness seemed to clear as they approached Yellowstone River.

"We are coming to Buffalo Valley," Bear said to Helen. "Carry your rifle just so." He showed her the Native way, balancing the barrel on the inside of her left elbow. "If there is more trouble, it will come here."

As they rode out on the level, a voice rang out. "So you come home, Itaxsca!"

Bear drew Horse to a halt. He waited. Out of the trees, a group of Crow warriors walked their horses toward him.

"Wolf That Runs," Bear said evenly.

"They say you have become some baheeitche of the Whites."

"It would seem so," replied Bear. "I hunt the Samson."

"You have developed balls indeed," said Wolf That Runs. "We hunt his men."

"There are twelve fewer for you to be concerned about," replied Bear.

A dry smile came over the face of Wolf That Runs. "There are twenty that will ride no more by our attack," said Wolf. "The Samson is losing his edge. Two more days and you will find him. Then two baheeitches will bump heads. Go with care my friend." Wolf That Runs reined in his horse and the four warriors thundered off down the trail.

"And that is a friend of yours?" questioned Helen.

"He is my cousin; my mother's sister's son," Bear replied. "We grew up together in the same village."

They rode on; the mountains faded to the horizon in the west. The rolling plains to the east. The wind blew cold and when they camped, the only fuel they could find was buffalo dung. It smelled very bad as it burned.

"I hate skat fires," said Bear. "It's a stinky way to keep warm."

Dog did not seem to mind as he hunkered down near the fire.

"Have you ever wondered if the horses get tired of standing?" Helen asked absentmindedly.

Bear laughed. "They lay down when they've had enough. Tomorrow we will find the Samson. You'd better sleep."

The day was dark, even though there was not a cloud in the sky. A shadow seemed to have come over the land and it became deeper as Bear and Helen drew near the ranch of Samson. They had passed a few traders with empty wagons on the way. They all looked discouraged and would not meet Bear's eyes.

Forty miles east of the Shoshone River they came upon it. A series of well-built ranch houses surrounded by a fog of darkness.

"What evil is this?" Bear said to himself.

They rode forward, and Horse was uneasy; only the steady hand of Bear kept his calm. Dog whined, his tail between his legs.

Suddenly, out of the mist, shots rang out. Bear heard Helen wince and say, "Oh!" She was shot. Bear took his rifle out and returned fire. A wall of darkness was pushed toward him from the main house. His mind was hard put to think clearly. He reached for his silver ring and took it out of his medicine pouch. He slipped it on his finger and the blue hazy fire appeared all around him.

"You all right?" he called to Helen.

"Yeah, it's just a scratch," he heard her reply.

"Samson!" Bear yelled. "I am a federal officer. Lay down your weapons and surrender."

The answer was plain; "Go to hell you Crow son-of-a bitch! Come in and get me!"

As Bear inched forward he realized this was the old Barlow place. He'd been in and out of here as a boy many times.

"Barlow!" he yelled, "Is that you?"

"Yep, that's me!" came the reply.

"Why are you doing this?"

"Arnell is dead and it's your tribe's fault!" came the answer.

Arnell was the gentle settler woman who had taught Bear to read English.

"I got Kachina medicine and it's got a hold of me."

Kachina medicine was potent Navajo medicine and it did not belong in Crow land.

"Put down your guns!" Bear yelled again.

The wind began to blow. Lightning flashed, and spirits flew. It was bizarre. It was Helen that broke the spell. She carefully balanced her gun on the middle of Horse's back and fired.

"Unnngh!" cried Barlow.

The ring shone brightly, angry spirits screamed around them and then all was quiet.

Bear and Helen approached the man slumped on the porch. Helen had shot him dead between the eyes. It was over.

"God Almighty," said Bear. "It's old Emmett Barlow. What the hell possessed him?"

They looked around and the whole cabin was filled with blankets, guns, and cans of poisoned flour. On the table was a small book amidst the ragged disarray. A picture of Arnell was propped up on a stack of books and an uneaten plate of food lay beside it.

Bear was amazed. He remembered coming here. He was nine or ten summers old. Arnell, Emmett's wife, had the

Native kids in to teach them English, and a few like Bear, to read.

"I think I found something," said Helen. She was holding her left arm inside her shirt babying the bullet wound in her arm. "It's his diary," she said. "It's fascinating. Listen."

"July 7th - Arnell is dying. Can't stop the fever. I told her not to let that damned Crow kid in here. Now she's got it. The sickness.

July 11th - She's so weak can't stop it. Got to do something.

July 13th - Arnell is gone. Died in the night. All is blackness in front of me. Damn it! I will get my revenge.

August 2nd - A wagon with a Navajo woman came in. She had some kind of medicine. Said I should call Kachina Spirits to clean the land of those damned Crows.

August 15th - Called the first spirits to me. I feel powerful. I can do anything strong, like Samson in the Bible. Collecting diseased blankets from dead wagon train. Trade to Crow. Hah! That'll show 'em!

September 6th - Can't control the Kachina spirits. They have a hold on me. It's evil, nothing less.

September 15th - The only way out is death. I have done great evil. Bear is coming. He will settle this issue!"

Helen paused and took a deep breath. "Seems like he knew you were after him."

Bear looked around, darkness still hovered inside the cabin and he remembered it as a child. He walked over to a kerosene lamp that was burning in the corner. He grabbed it and threw it down. The fire went up; it burned hungrily, consuming the inside of the cabin.

Helen and Bear walked quickly out to the porch and looked at Barlow's body. His dead face seemed to fall against the bone, as if he'd died long ago.

"Let the fire take him," Bear said. "This evil is done."

They watched from a distance as the cabin was consumed, Barlow with it. When the roof fell in, an audible sigh went up in all the lands around. Emmett had his revenge but paid for it with his life.

"That damned rifle bullet hurt," said Helen, finally looking at her wound.

"Let's see it," Bear said. He forgot his ring was still on his finger and as he touched her arm a blue glow surrounded them.

"Ahh!" moaned Helen. "What are you doing?"

"Sorry," he said. "Let's take a look." The wound was small and to their surprise, it started to bubble and close. Inside three or four minutes there was only a red mark on her arm.

"Better put this thing away," Bear said as he returned the ring to its leather pouch. Helen blinked in amazement.

Even Ossiaro was wrong about the Samson. Emmett had been there all the time. Old Emmett Barlow," he thought. His wife Arnell was such a good woman. She had taken in illiterate Native children and helped them learn to read. A few, like himself, made it a passion.

Emmett had embraced Dark Kachina medicine that had come from the South and turned him into the Samson. It was a sad thing he thought, remembering Arnell and her gift of words to the Crow children.

X

The cabin collapsed under the burning fire. It consumed everything hungrily, and as Bear and Helen turned to go, there was a long hollow moan that encompassed the whole valley. The darkness lifted; it was done.

Four Ponies met them on the trail as the two approached his village. He was smiling broadly at them.

"They are dancing in your honor," he said. "The darkness is gone."

Bear nodded in recognition of the honor, but still he was afraid of the silver ring and the power he carried. It carefully rested in his medicine pouch on his chest. He would forget it again. He did not want to tempt fate or use it until it was absolutely necessary. The dance was beautiful. Helen was honored by the tribe as well, and when all was said and done, Helen and Bear found themselves back in Forsythe in room number 9. Helen stretched out on the bed and smiled. "Come here, you big Crow warrior."

The Passing of Blue Knife

Bear's gun gleamed in the sunlight, hot after being fired so many times. The street was littered with dead and dying men groaning and gasping their last breath of air before meeting the Great Mystery.

Smoke filled the still morning air and Bear waited for the law to show up. It was always this way.

"What the hell is going on here?" shouted out a voice.

"Did that damned injun do it again?"

It was town Marshall Joseph Todd that stood before Bear, a shotgun pointed at his head.

"What went on here?" He growled.

"Arizona Bob, Wyatt Belcher, Tom Crane," said Bear slowly. "All wanted."

"I forgot," said Marshall Todd. "You're all legal and everything." He did not like the fact that Bear Itaxsca was a Native and had been sworn in at Fort Smith as a Federal Marshall and licensed bounty hunter.

Bear sat there waiting for the mob to gather, legal executions were frowned on by the citizenry, especially when it was a Native doing the killing.

"Come along to the office," said Marshall Todd. "These guys were right popular around here. I don't want your scalp to be on someone's lodge pole before sunset. And," he added angrily, "I don't want no more killing to save your wretched hide."

Bear was silent. He stood and followed the Marshall to his office. Dog followed, growling all the way. "Shut up, Dog" Bear said in a low voice.

They walked quickly up the street and around the corner, Bear leading Horse, and Dog at his heels. Bear tied Horse at the front porch and patted him on the neck gently.

'This is getting old' thought Bear to himself. 'It's always like this. Do your duty, then have the people you saved spit on you for doing it.'

"Okay," said Marshall Todd. "I will get the paper on those boys your dropped and be back with your money." He shook his head as he left. "You stay put until it's done, then I want you out of town, pronto!"

The process took a couple of hours. They wanted Bear's bounty number 96994, authorization from the State Office and Bear's signature on several documents. After that Marshall Todd put $1,500 into Bear's hand and said, "Now git."

Bear had found that friends were few in this business that Crispin the judge in Fort Smith had given him. He seemed to be the shadow of death to everyone he met. The only haven he had was with Helen, the owner of the Silver Dollar Saloon in Durango. She had made up her mind that Bear was hers and that was that. It felt kind of like being owned by someone. She was so sweet to him even though he had a problem being objective about it. He remembered what she had said after the Samson episode.

"Why don't you come back and run the Silver Dollar with me? You'd have a place and a ready-made family. And," she paused to let the thought sink in, "I love you!"

Bear walked to the telegraph office and wired his money to the Bank in San Francisco. It was a lengthy process, but finally sums were exchanged. It was blood money he knew, but he had close to $50,000 in that Bank. By accounts, out here he was the richest redskin in these parts.

Bear went to the store and got supplies for the journey, then back to Durango. Twenty pounds of jerky, oats for the horse, nuts and herbs and tobacco. He watered Horse down and Dog wagged his tail with a mouth full of jerky Bear had given him.

Bear felt totally alone. No one wanted to be his friend. He mounted Horse and rode North.

The wind blew cold from the North. It was March and Bear knew there could be snow at any time. Daylight started to fade; it was time to camp.

The land was alive with deer and rabbits; Dog caught a small varmint for their dinner.

Up ahead he saw the rock face that he knew had a small traveler's cave in it. He hoped it wasn't occupied.

"We'll camp there," he said to Horse. "We won't freeze inside the cave."

It took them about two hours to get to the decaying rock face that held the cave.

"Hello the camp!" Bear shouted. All he heard was the icy blowing of the wind. The trail led down a slight hill, slippery in the March thawing wetness. Horse picked his way down it carefully. They came at last to the traveler's cave. Its mouth was open to let all three of them shelter in it. He checked for other inhabitants but found it empty. There was a small fire ring, rocks laid in a circle near the cave mouth, and dry rock with a sandy floor. It was an ideal shelter for a cold weather traveler like himself. Bear had on a buffalo robe coat and two pairs of socks. Still, it wasn't enough to keep out the fingers of the cold North wind.

The sun was setting, and he knew a fire would be much needed. He looked around and found that a thoughtful traveler had left some dry kindling in the corner. He gathered scrub wood he found outside the cave then a small deadfall tree into the cave. Soon it made a merry blaze.

The storm came - snow, howling wind and rain, but Bear, Horse and Dog hunkered down inside the cave and let it do its worst. Bear laid his rifle across his lap just in case they had visitors that were caught in the storm.

Three days the storm raged and only upon the third night did Bear smell a shift in the air. The fourth day dawned bright and clear.

"Looks like we can dig our way out of this hole." He said to Dog. More than a foot of snow had fallen at the cave's entryway. He was just putting the saddle back on Horse when he heard a shout from outside.

"Itaxsca!" He grabbed his rifle, cocked it and laid it cross ways in his arms.

"Come ahead!" He yelled in reply.

Out of the low mist that hugged the ground there appeared a lone warrior, riding a brown and white paint horse. The warrior was wrapped in a buffalo robe and carried his rifle crossways just as Bear did and ready for anything. He was tall and wore his hair loose with three feathers attached to stick straight up in the back. The man's face was expressionless.

"Wolf That Runs," said Bear recognizing him straight away. "You are a long way from Crow lands."

"I was sent to find you," Wolf replied.

"It is good to see you," Bear said. "But you never were a traveler. What has happened?"

"Your father, Blue Knife, is dying," said Wolf. "He would have you by his side when he goes to the Great Spirit.

"He who turned his back on me when I fought for the Whites," Bear said, remembering the scene in the teepee. Blue Knife had turned his back on Bear, exiling him from the tribe.

"Itaxsca," said Wolf That Runs. "Things change at the end, and he loves you above all. I will say no more. Are you coming?"

"Where is his teepee now?" Bear asked.

"Beyond Eagle Mountain," replied Wolf. "Hard up against the Lakota lands. It has been very difficult for him."

“I will come.” Bear said. He remembered then the last death he had been in attendance for - his grandfather.

II

Bear swung into the saddle and headed north. It would be a long journey. He wondered if Wolf That Runs would stay with him to be his companion or not. He was sent to tell Bear what was happening, not to be his travel companion.

“How far are you with me?” Bear asked.

“My lodge is just south of the Yellowstone,” Wolf said. “I will leave you when we reach there.”

They rode on in silence. Bear was comforted by the presence of Wolf That Runs. It threw him back into the days before he went to fight for the Whites; then the two warriors had been a swift and silent hunting party.

Three days later they came to a small town on the edge of the Mountain Trail. The Whites had settled throughout Crow lands. Bear could not remember the town being there five years before.

“What is this town?” Bear asked Wolf.

“Another scar on the land,” Wolf replied. “They pop up like pimples on a sick man’s face.”

“Ah well,” Sighed Bear. “The years pass, and things change. Let us go in. We need provisions.”

"You go in," said Wolf. "I will meet you at Antelope Creek beyond." He nodded toward the north. "I do not do well with the Whites."

"As you wish," Bear replied. "I have learned how to walk among them."

Bear stood beside Horse as they entered the small town. The sign said, 'Welcome to Boulder Creek, Population 678.'

Bear tied Horse on the railing in front of the general store and went in. There was a sign on the door stating, "We do not serve Indians." Bear drew his gun, cocked it and laid it on the counter. His badge gleamed in the morning light and it was plain he meant business.

"Don't you read?" asked the scowling clerk. "Now git outta here!" Then the man stopped, seeing the gun on the counter and the badge on Bear's chest.

"What is it you want?" asked the clerk.

"I want traveling provisions," Bear said calmly. "Twenty pounds of jerky, some oats for the horse, and tobacco." Bear threw down two twenty-dollar gold pieces. "That ought to take care of it. I'll be back in an hour to pick it up."

The clerk glared at him but scooped the gold up and put it in his register.

"Why is it always like this?" he asked himself. Why does the White's prejudice run so deep? Why did he have to bully his way into a general store? It never seemed right.

He walked, straight backed and steady, to a tent in the middle of town where a sign hung – 'Ma's Eatery.' He was not about to exist on jerky and oats all the way to the Shoshone

River. He stared at the Rockies, red in the morning sunrise to his left. He was too far from Helen. He thought of Helen Hardin, the beautiful owner of the Silver Dollar Saloon in Durango. His mind went to her as he walked. She was about five foot four, slim body with China white skin and full auburn hair. Her smile spread over her face with dimples on each side. It made Bear smile to himself as he recalled her making herself Bear's woman, whether he liked it or not. He liked it.

He approached the entrance to Ma's and a large man barred his way. The man crossed his huge muscular arms across his chest.

"We don't serve Injuns here, mister," He barked. "You got to go round the back."

Bear looked him hard in the eye. "Which way is that?" Bear asked.

"You all go round that way," the man said, pointing to his left. He was fat and balding, smelling of grease and as though he hadn't bathed for a year. His grimy vest shone greasy black in the sun. Bear guessed he was illiterate too.

"Thank you," said Bear, and walked around to the back. He had no mind for a fight today.

There were some scruffy looking Pawnee standing in line. They looked like they hadn't eaten good for a year. One man, who had once been a proud warrior, stepped forward.

"Cho da cha," he said.

"A choa," replied Bear. "What are you eating today?"

"Whatever bits they give out," the man replied. "We are not fussy."

"Sit down here brothers," Bear said. His heart went out to those in need. "You will eat well today."

He whistled for the cook, who stuck his head out and growled, "What'd you want?"

"Ham and eggs and potatoes all around," said Bear.

"We don't give that meal to Injuns."

"How 'bout forty dollars in gold?" Offered Bear.

The cook's eyes bugged out and he wiped his dirty hand across his face. He'd never seen forty dollars in gold Bear guessed.

"You betcha," the cook said, and in the blink of an eye he rolled a big ham, twenty or so eggs, and badly done potatoes out to the Pawnee. He snatched the two twenty-dollar gold pieces greedily from Bear's hand.

"Good eatin'," the cook said.

There were five Pawnee Natives. They looked proud and sat there looking at, but not touching the food.

"The Crow are generous," said the one warrior. "Would you like to use one of our women for a while?"

Bear didn't expect that. He slashed his hand across his chest in a "no" gesture. "I will take your knife," Bear said.

The Pawnee smiled and gave him a small, well-made knife in a leather sheath.

"Good trade," said Bear, and he sat down beside them. The trading of the knife had paid for the food and their human dignity. They ate together as equals.

After Bear had eaten he went back to the general store, collected his provisions and headed out of town. He met his cousin Wolf That Runs on the banks of the Little Antelope Creek and they continued on their journey north.

As they rode Bear studied his cousin. He was hardly older than Bear, but he looked worn, a face like old saddle leather, scars from battle, and hard, unyielding hands. He had found no place in life. Life itself was a hard duty. They rode on into the misty cold morning.

Two days later they came to the edge of the Yellowstone. It was a frosty, calm day. The horses smelled sweaty and their hooves rang hollow on the ground. Dog was even quiet.

"I go west from here," said Wolf That Runs. "You will find your father's teepee in about six days – north, past Eagle Mountain. May the wind be at your back, Itaxsca."

"For you also," replied Bear as he saw Wolf That Runs fade slowly down the western trail.

III

Bear crossed the Yellowstone River avoiding the geysers and sulfur lakes. The land opened out into a grand panorama, mountains to the west, plains to the east. On and on it stretched until he could see the faint curve of the earth. The wind blew and never stopped. He had forgotten how the voice of Wakan Tanka spoke to him in these places, and now he could hear the Great Spirit clearly.

March was on its way to April and he finally came to Eagle Mountain and Shoshone River. The land seemed bare of Crow and it wasn't until he came into Shoshone Valley that he saw any sign of villages. The villages were scattered thinly in that cold area. He stopped at one village seeking food and news of Blue Knife's location.

"Cho da cha," he hailed a passing warrior.

"A choa," the man replied.

"I am the Itaxsca," Bear said. "I am searching for my father's camp."

The warrior eyed him in silence and then spoke. "Up past the draw on the other side of the mountain," he said. "I hope you are not too late," the man continued. "It is said that he is dying. Go into this village. They know more there."

It had been a long time since Bear had entered a Crow village. He rode slowly and cautiously as he watched the way the Natives looked at him. He was trail rough, but more than that, he was dressed as a White man. He rounded the first teepee and a voice called out to him.

He turned to see a woman he knew was called Moon. Moon had been his friend and ally as they grew up.

"Bear Itaxsca!" shouted the woman. "Bear!"

She was short, just over five-foot tall, and had put on weight, but her dark eager eyes caught his. She ran up to Horse and reached up, hugging Bear's leg. "I thought I'd never see you again! Where have you been?"

Most of the village women who were watching exchanged looks and were laughing at Moon's excitement.

"Moon!" Bear said. He was glad to see a friendly face. "Why are you here in this village?"

"My father married me off to an old pig named Far Elk." She said, almost spitting out his name.

Bear shook his head. "I didn't think your father could make you do anything," he joked. "I look for some food and direction. But I must let the bacheeitche know that I am in his village."

"That would be Grey Hawk," Moon said. "This is his band of Crow."

"Just go over - well, hell," she said. "I'll take you."

Moon swung herself up in back of Bear and said, "Giddy-up!" It was one of the rare times Horse smiled and Dog wagged his tail.

She slid off Horse's rump right before the last teepee in the row.

"It's Bear," she squealed. "It's Bear Itaxsca."

An older Crow man, regal looking, poked his head out of the teepee. He had the look of arrogance like a man that had been disturbed from an important task. Grey Elk was nearly as tall as Bear, fifty years old and straight backed. He was in his prime and Bear could see his muscular body underneath the blanket he had wrapped around himself. His chiseled features and piercing eyes measured Bear in a glance.

"Cho da cha," he said. "What brings the Son of Blue Knife to my village?"

Bear looked him directly in the eye. "Trail Weariness," he said. "I seek my father's village, but he has moved."

"I hear it is beyond the Mountain. That is the rumor," said Grey Elk. "So, you stay for a while, or just tonight?"

"Just tonight," replied Bear.

"My teepee is open to you," said Grey Elk. He turned and went inside. That simple action told Bear it was a very reserved welcome. Everyone knew that Bear had been exiled by his father. It was a cold welcome, but at least Bear wasn't sprouting arrows in his back.

Moon leaned forward and spoke in Bear's ear. "That was a cold shoulder," she said. "You can sleep with me." She looked hopeful, but Bear shook his head.

"I do not want my throat cut in the night," he laughed. "You are a joined woman. Horse and Dog and I will camp in the tall grass down by the river."

Horse was very happy. He grazed on the new March grass and all was right for a change. This was his country too. The smell of the north wind brought memories to him of running free and of the time he found his master Bear, and they had become bonded.

The village women threw out buffalo bones for the dogs, and a mixture of chokecherry and meat for the dogs to fill their bellies. Dog had his nose right in there, plus a fat rabbit he had chased down. It smelled of home to Bear, and for the first time in years, he felt safe within the tribe.

Bear went down to the river and stripped, then dove into the freezing March river. He felt the stain of travel loosen and fall away. It was so cold his skin turned blue, but he was home, not his village, but this was his country. He thought about what his father would say to him. He was a different person from the boy who had left to fight slavery with the Whites. So many things had occurred like water that had flowed under the bridge. He was the Itaxsca now, not just Bear.

Bear stood naked in the gentle spring sunshine, drying off in the high grass.

"You are beautiful," said a woman's voice behind him. It was Moon. She stood there looking at him like he was a buffalo steak she had a mind to eat. Unashamed, she slipped off her dress and stood naked before him.

"Make love to me, Bear." She whispered. "My husband is away on the hunt. I want to feel you all around me!"

They fell down in the tall grass and she was in complete rapture as Bear made love to her.

"I have made an enemy today!" Bear said.

"Do you think I will tell the old bastard? She said with a smile. "I've been waiting six years to have you. That old man can wait in line after you. You are first!"

Moon covered herself and kissed Bear deeply. "Thank you," she whispered. "Maybe we will have a son. Then I can look upon you when you are gone."

Bear said nothing. He had tumbled his childhood sweetheart in her own village. 'It's time for me to head north or I may be full of arrows.' He thought.

Aloud he said, "I will go with the rising sun. We probably won't meet for a long while. Please have lots of babies and be happy Moon."

She looked at the ground and said very quietly, "I love you Bear Itaxsca. Try to stay alive."

IV

It was the pearl grey of dawn. The full moon was still shining as the sun made the Rockies blush to red. The light cloud bank was orange and black with a low rumble of distant thunder that told him he'd better make some time on the trail.

Horse stumbled along in the rocky scree that slipped beneath his hooves. He made great effort and pulled himself and his rider to the safety of the plateau trail. The trail led around the foot of Eagle Mountain. Bear wondered why his father had chosen this remote area to locate his people. Beyond the mountain was the expanse of Montana and the Lakota Sioux. They were sworn enemies of the Crow. Bear paid attention to the trail; he would leave deep thinking until he reached camp.

Half way down the mountain Bear saw a small wisp of smoke, campfire most likely right by the trail. As he neared the smoke plume his medicine bag started to tingle. He knew it was possibly danger.

He approached the camp carefully. Four men and a woman sat around a blazing fire attempting to get warm. They were White folks who seemed travel worn but not an evil sort. Their coats were dirty and torn; the floppy hats they wore were full of holes. Their jeans had patched pockets. The woman was covered by a huge buffalo coat.

"Hello the camp!" Bear shouted.

They jumped as though they'd been scared out of their wits.

"Who are you?" shouted one of the men.

"Bear," he said. "Bear Itaxsca."

"Are you friendly?" asked the camper.

"Yeah, you can put your guns up," said Bear.

"Come ahead then." The man said.

Bear walked Horse right into the camp. The fire was bright and warm. Dog did not wag his tail.

"What are you folks doin' so far off the trail?" asked Bear as a second man handed him a cup of coffee. It was rich and bitter right off the campfire grill.

"We was prospecting, said the one man. "Name's Martin Shievers." He held out his hand for Bear to shake.

"Bear Itaxsca," repeated Bear, taking his hand. "Had a bad time out here?"

"Yeah," said the other. "No gold up here. Only rocks and injuns."

"We're on our way to Great Falls, then on to Iowa," said Martin.

"That's a far piece to travel," said Bear. He suspected these people were wanted by the law, but it was none of his business right now. "You'd best take the trail to the right, a little further down from here," said Bear. He downed the coffee. "It's easier going that direction. I'll be movin' on," he said. "Thanks for the coffee."

Around the group there was some scattering. "Good trails to you," he said but Bear took it for what it was. At this point he hoped they'd get away and not involve him.

It was six hours of riding and Bear was walking horse through a gentle meadow of spring grasses when he heard someone call him from afar.

" Itaxsca," said the voice. "Bear Itaxsca."

He recognized it was another woman he had known since childhood – White Horn Maxon. He saw her standing on a hill waving her coat at him.

"Maxon is that you?" he yelled.

"Yes!" said the voice. "I'm coming over to you."

Bear remembered her, a woman of his village that had been with a White trapper named Eli Maxon. She was beloved of the tribe and Bear had liked her from the beginning.

Soon there was the pounding of hooves and she rode into the glade where Bear waited for her. She was all breathless, and steam was coming from the horse's mouth.

"Maxon, what's your hurry?" asked Bear.

"I was told Wolf That Runs had found you and that you were near," she said. "Blue Knife dies," she went on. "He calls for his son. Hurry!"

They mounted and rode hard for almost twenty miles, until the horses were worn out. There at the very foot of Eagle Mountain was the village of Blue Knife Itaxsca, Bear's father.

The teepees were arranged in a circle around the largest teepee in the center. It had a blue sash sewn on it. It was Blue Knife's home. Bear's heart was in his mouth as he pulled back the flap of buffalo hide that was the door. His father, grey and sunken, lay by the fire, wrapped in buffalo robes. Bear's mother, Marsilla, was beside him weeping. She got up and came to Bear. She drew back her arm and slapped him across the face.

"Why hadn't you come?" she cried. Then she hugged Bear, snuggling into his chest like a baby.

"Don't you remember, Mother?" he asked her. "Didn't you exile me for choosing to fight for the Whites?"

"The house of his spirit crumbles," she said, ignoring Bear's accusation. "He would see his son again. Come." Marsilla took Bear's hand and drew him to his father's bedside.

"Your son has returned, husband," she said and laid Bear's hand in the hand of Blue Knife.

V

Blue Knife Itaxsca opened his heavy eye lids and a smile passed over his face. "It is good that you are here," he said. "To see me off into the other world."

Blue Knife reached up and touched the medicine bag that hung around Bear's neck.

"You have the ring," he rasped. "It was good the Itaxsca gave it to you. You are strong, my son."

Blue Knife's eyes seemed to see far away and there was the sound of tingling in the lodge. For a moment the ring gave off a gentle blue haze that filled the teepee. Bear's father took one last breath and was gone. Bear could see his father's shadow as it lifted from the body and drifted into smallness and disappeared. Marsilla broke into tears and held her husband's hand close to her breast.

Bear rose and walked out of the teepee. He said to all those who had gathered around his father's teepee using his father's name aloud for the last time, "Blue Knife Itaxsca has passed."

There was a great keening from the women. The men sat silent and composed, seemingly unmoved, but some lowered their heads. The sorrow and grieving of the People was palpable.

"You are the Itaxsca now," said one of them. "The tribe needs you." Bear did not speak. He could not lead the tribe. His soul was no longer only Crow. He had lived among the Whites too long. How could he lead a people?

"Who is your Holy Man?" Bear asked.

"Mantani," said another man.

"Then," said Bear firmly, you will follow Mantani. And I will take my father's body to the four winds."

Bear carried his father's body to the plateau that over looked the village and faced the rising sun. He erected a burial scaffold raised up off the ground. With the help of several younger braves, he put lifted his father's body on it. Bear's spirit was ever attuned to the rising sun and the four winds. This would be his father's resting place. Bear put all of his father's prized possessions on the bier with him, and lastly covered him with the white buffalo robe of a chief.

When the task was completed he returned to the village and said to Marsilla, "Mother, you will come with me to Durango. I have a woman I want you to meet."

VI

It was twenty days after the passing of Blue Knife that two very tired travelers walked their horses into Durango, Colorado. They dismounted in front of the Silver Dollar Saloon and Bear went inside.

"I have a woman for you to meet." Bear said to a surprised Helen Hardin. "Her name is Marsilla, my mother."

Helen beamed with excitement.

"Cho da Cha," said Helen, hopefully waiting for an embrace. Marsilla looked around her in the saloon. She was not comfortable with White lodges and White people. She looked at Helen and thought, "But this woman...."

Epilogue

VII

Nine months later a small Crow woman struggled in birthing. Her mother was her midwife.

"Now push, baby girl!" Said the mother, "Push."

A strong new voice was heard, crying loudly. It was a son.

Moon smiled as she held the newborn in her arms. "Bear I shall name you," she whispered. "You shall know your father."

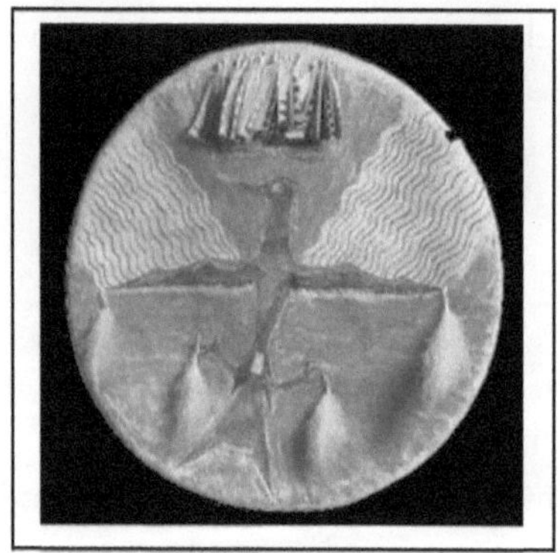

Bear Itaxsca's Revenge

I

The courtroom was dark, the first shadows of evening crowding in on a lonely desk. One light shone as Judge W.T. Crispin sat there. He was going through the day's cases trying to reach a decision on some of the tougher ones, cases he'd set aside for further thought.

He was startled at the rattle of the chamber doors. "I don't want to be disturbed!" he shouted out. "Come back

Tomorrow."

There was no answer. Then quiet. He went back to work. Suddenly, with a great crash, all four chamber doors burst open and there stood four men guns in hand.

They cocked and fired wounding Judge Crispin mortally. The judge jerked in his chair, blood flowing all over his desk. He was soon to be dead.

"The Confederacy will rise again!" shouted the man in the middle. They ran for their horses and beat a hasty retreat up the streets of Fort Smith, past the courthouse and into the night.

Judge Crispin struggled with his last breath to write something with his dripping finger - "Assassins."

The Marshalls came to the court house next morning responding to a clerk beside himself with excitement.

"They've shot the judge!" he kept screaming.

When the Marshalls arrived, they came upon the grisly scene of W.T. Crispin slumped over his desk, pen still in hand, with one dying word written - "Assassins". They sent for the military.

The military man, Captain Jarod Keen, sealed the building and put his men at work to find a clue.

"Who would do a thing like this?" he asked himself.

At that moment one of his men came running up. "Look what I found!" he said, holding up a small flag - stars and bars. "The south will rise again boys," he said shaking his head in disgust. "I should have known. We'll never find 'em," said the soldier. "They've got friends everywhere."

"I know someone," Keen said. His thoughts went back to the war and the marvelous leader of Morgan's troops. He was a Native. His name was Bear.

Bear sat up straight in bed. Helen Hardin lay softly snoring to his left and Dog was in his corner sleeping calmly.

Something was wrong. Bear's medicine bag hung around his neck, stung in his chest as the feeling of danger filled the air around him. His hand was already holding his pistol; the hammer was cocked.

"What's going on?" he asked himself. "Everything seems alright here." Soon there came a knock on his door.

"Mr. Bear," called the voice of Henry, the telegraph boy. "Come down to the office quick!"

"Ho boy," said Bear. "What's the trouble?"

"There's a telegram for you down at the office from the Army," replied Henry. "They want your immediate reply."

"I'll be along in a bit," said Bear. "Tell them I'll be

there in a while."

Henry thumped away down the hall and Bear slid out of bed shaking loose all the cobwebs that remained in his head.

Helen stirred and stretched. "Mmmm?" she said. "What gets you up Bear?"

"My medicine bag just went crazy on me and Henry the telegraph boy says I have an urgent message from the Army," Bear replied. "I hope they haven't started the whole war up again."

"I'm coming with you" said Helen.

"Stay here and sleep," said Bear. "I won't do anything till I tell you about it."

"O.K." she said as she slumped back under the covers. "But don't just leave. I want to know what's going on."

Bear finished dressing and, as usual, he was an imposing figure of a man. Six foot one, flat brimmed hat, vest, guns stuck in his sash. He was a man to step aside for.

"Dog!" he commanded, and the Coyote-Australian Shepard was at his heels.

Down the hall and stairs he went never making a sound. Walking quietly was a skill he had acquired as a boy. It came second nature to him now.

Out the doors of the Silver Dollar saloon and down the street of Durango, Bear noticed it was one of those dusty yellow days. The dust was everywhere; it turned yellow in the morning sun. His footsteps seemed hollow on the hard, dry dirt. It was a day to be ready for anything.

He sniffed the dusty air and caught no scent of water. It was bone dry.
As he approached the telegraph office he saw Henry, a skinny young boy, peering out the window anxiously.

"He's here!" he said.

"Urgent message from the Army," said Elmer. Elmer had ridden the wire as long as anybody could remember. In fact, he and his son Henry were the only telegraphers within a hundred miles.

Bear looked at the paper. It read: *Crispin murdered. Need you here to track them down. Come quickly. Captain Jarod Keene.*

Bear took it all in, nodded and crumbled the envelope in his right hand then left without a word.

Bear knew Keene. He was the eager lieutenant that was always getting in his way during the war. He remembered having to teach him how to fight.

But to murder Crispin and for what reason? Bear was

compelled to go. He felt a deep sorrow at this man's passing, right to the core of his heart. Judge Crispin had honored him, respected him as a soldier and as a man. He would not let this go unavenged!

The quickest way to Fort Smith was by train and Bear was on it before the day passed.

"I'm coming with you," Helen said again when he told her. "That was a beastly thing to have happened."

"No Woman," said Bear calmly. "This is a journey for Bear alone. And besides, I need you here to watch over my mother and Emma and Charlie."

By now Helen had learned when Bear meant business. "O.K. I'll hold down the fort," she replied. "But you take care. I don't want to lose you even by accident."

Bear went to the stables to retrieve Horse.

The keeper, old Long John Shorty, said, "He ain't here right now."

Bear knew what he meant and stepped out the back sliding doors, letting out a big whistle. In the distance he heard a great neighing and soon Horse came thundering up, mane flying, hooves clicking with glee.

"That damned horse of yours won't stay in the barn,"

said Shorty. "He is always wantin' to run free. Never goes far, but he can't stand being cooped up. He comes fer his oats and to get bedded down," he continued. "Elsewise he's out in that damned field."

Bear laughed. "That is because he is a Crow horse. Free to the Wind, Shorty. The Wind is his master. I am just his friend."

Horse came up and nuzzled Bear's neck, ready for his saddle and gear.

"Horse, my friend," he said quietly. "Are you ready for another journey?"

Horse stamped and shook his head. By Bear's reckoning Horse was six or seven years old and in his prime. He remembered the colt he found alone in a field so many years ago. Horse had been wild but let Bear approach. Bear came to him each day for a long while. After several days he brought a skin to throw on Horse's back, led him around, talked to him, and then mounted him. It was a gentle way of breaking him in for Horse would die fighting any man before letting himself be hard broke. It was a partnership, a bond that could not be broken.

Bear slung the saddle on him, tightened the cinch strap, and swung up on Horse's back - a magnificent warrior he looked. "Thank you for caring for him," Bear said to Shorty.

"No problem Bear," Shorty replied. Bear dug into his pocket and found ten dollars in gold. Shorty smiled and knew he would eat well today.

Bear turned and went toward the rail head, some five miles away.

II

There was no station there as he approached, just a landing with a lean-to shelter thrown up for bad weather.

The west and east bound trains shared the same track with a side branch for loading. The wind blew a mournful tune as it whipped the dust around, causing little dust devils out on the plain.

To the east were the mountains that caught the first rosy glow of dawn. Bear could see the trees crowded, as though they were marching up the sides of the foothills to where the tree line stopped.

"We'll catch those guys," he said to Horse. "It burns me that such a good man was cut down in such a fashion."

His mind went back over the scenes of death and

destruction he witnessed in that damn war. "What were they fighting for?" he asked himself. "Nothing but the right to hold slaves? No, it must have been a larger issue."

He heard the east bound train coming and put out the flag that told the engineer to pick
up passengers or goods. Soon the train pulled in, slowing to a metal screeching stop.

"Animals?" the engineer yelled.

"Horse and dog," replied Bear.

"Ok, three cars back. I'll pull forward for ya."

The train ground forward slowly. The door of the animal car slid open. Horse had done this before. He knew it was an awful way to travel but with Bear leading him he went peacefully to water, hay and oats in the animal car.

"Hold still now," said Bear in a soft voice. "We gotta go a long way in a short time; this is the best way."

Bear left the rein lines loose and shut the door. He knew Horse was nervous and he felt his anxiety, but some things were necessary.

Bear climbed into the passenger car with Dog behind him. The conductor, a small shriveled old man said, "Where you headed?"

"Fort Smith," replied Bear.

"That'll be ten dollars," he said.

Bear put a twenty-dollar gold piece in his hand. "For the animals too," he said.

"That's right enough and then some. Thank you, sir," said the conductor.

The seats were hard. Bear made himself as comfortable as possible, leaning on his saddle, relaxing his mind and putting in travel time. The chug and clank of the train on the rails was hypnotic and soon Bear was napping, unaware of the passage of hours.

It was about six o'clock when the train made an abrupt stop. Bear looked up and listened. There was a great deal of shouting in the car ahead of him. Instinctively he drew his 36's and walked slowly ahead into the other car.

He saw three men, masked and armed, trying to rob the passengers. The men looked desperate.

"You fellas need something?" asked Bear quietly.

"Stick 'em up Injun," said one, pointing his gun at Bear.

"No," replied Bear. "You guys better take a powder - now."

They seemed a ragged bunch of thieves. He did not want to kill them for their sad effort.

"Take your treasure and leave," Bear said sternly.

Then it happened. The short mouthy one drew down on Bear. There were three quick shots from Bear's 36's and all three men lay dead on the floor.

Women screamed, and the men seemed to recover their courage, grabbing at the bodies to recover their own possibles from the dead ruffians.

Bear walked forward. He surmised these were not all the thieves. He was right. Four more had the engineer at gun point and were searching for the pay that was being hauled from Denver to Fort Smith.

Bear didn't say a word as he caught up with them. He just shot, the smoke filling the air as the robbers dropped. His silent approach took them all by surprise.

It was done. The robbers lay dead, no longer a menace. The guy that was outside holding the horses was now headed for Montana. The engineer looked up, a look of relief on his face.

"Jesus be praised," he said. "You are the hero of the day."

"No," said Bear. "Just don't like thieves. Now can we get on our way?"

"Yes, yes," said the engineer. "Let's get outta here."

The brakeman had moved the tree off the tracks that the thieves had used to stop the train and he bounced back into the cab saying, "All good ahead. Let's roll!"

The brief adventure was over. They went on without a hitch. Bear settled down to listen to the steady clunk of wheels on the rails.

III

The train pulled into the Fort Smith train yard about midnight that same day. Bear was tired and went immediately to get Horse from the animal freight car. Horse seemed none the worse for wear.

Bear saddled him up and rode him around; a handful of oats made his apology for the cramped ride.

Bear went looking for a room to stay in. Fort Smith was a busy hub of trade and a great deal was going on even at night, compared to Durango. He walked into the first hotel he saw after stabling Horse, and they seemed to know him before he spoke a word. It was strange.

"I would like a room," he said. "Number eleven if possible."

"Yes sir, Mr. Itaxsca," said the clerk. "We already have it reserved for you."

Again it took Bear by surprise. He was used to having to bully his way into accommodations, but this was new.

"Captain Keene has room 11 reserved for you all over town," said the clerk. "Paid for by the Army. I 'spect he'll be down to see you in the morning."

All Bear could say was, "And dog."

The clerk just gave him the key and smiled.

Bear went through his room ritual he had learned in the army; door wedged by a chair, two sticks in the window. Guns at the ready. People had always hated a Native that was their equal and he expected they were out to get him. He didn't understand why he was usually hated and he could not understand preferential treatment either.

He crawled between the sheets exhausted, but he placed his gun under the pillow before sleeping. He slept well into the morning when a hard knock woke him. "Who is it?" he yelled.

"Captain Keene, Bear," the voice replied. "You gonna sleep all day?"

Bear was glad to hear his voice. He rolled out of bed and slipped his pants and boots on, then he picked the chair out from under the door knob and said, "Come on in."

Dog in the corner growled just a little, a stranger in his

room.

Keene was dressed in full riding gear, U.S. Cavalry style.

"God, you're pretty," chided Bear as the two embraced.

"You look like you've been livin' under the bridge," the other replied. "How goes it with you?" asked Keene.

"You know," replied Bear. "Makin' a living. How 'bout you?"

"They promoted me shortly after our Captain Morgan died," he said. "It was a shock at first, to be in command. But you adjust."

"We have a situation here," he continued. "It's that same old itch the Rebels have to scratch; restore the Confederacy. They go around assassinating public figures hoping to gear up the war again. They shot Crispin and now they've headed south toward Mexico to join up with Shelby and his boys."

"Sounds bigger than me," Bear said. "You'll be wanting a regiment to go after them."

"Yeah," said Keene. "But we got to find out where they're hiding first. That's your job."

"Sounds doable but it's gotta be my way," Bear said.

"White men are a bit clumsy in the bushes."

"That's what I figured," said Keene. "But find 'em you will. I know you and I can't think of anyone better suited to the task. You were also fond of Judge Crispin."

"Did they bury him yet?" asked Bear.

"Yeah, up on the hill behind the fort," said Keene.

Bear was silent. He finally said, "I will go and see him before we start."

Bear retrieved Horse from the stables and gave the keeper twenty dollars. There were few hills around Fort Smith. The single hill nearby was the one that had the federal cemetery. On the very top was a lone headstone that read, "Judge W. T. Crispin, killed in the line of duty."

"I will avenge you," Bear said. "Your spirit will rest."

Bear took out tobacco and prayed to the four winds and the Great Spirit. He blessed Crispin's grave. He would find the men who did this.

Later he asked Captain Keene, "Do you have any idea which way they went?"

"The nearest we can figure, Bear, they were off to Mexico to join Joe Shelby. He has an army of Confederates still there waiting to renew the war."

"I will go south then and see what I can see."

"Go careful," Captain Keene said. "That's Comanche country."

"I will speak to them." Bear said. "They will know what passes in their land."

"Will they help a Crow?" asked Captain Keene.

"More readily than the soldiers," said Bear. "They hate Whites far more than a distant tribe they've never heard of. They will know where the Confederates are."

Bear Itaxsca was on the hunt now. If the Confederates fled they would have to go through Iron Shirt's country. They may have even traded with the Comanches. He would first visit Iron Shirt and his people. They knew everything about who went through their land.

Before he left he asked Keene for two fine horses, a gift for Iron Shirt. The horses in tow, he left Fort Smith south west into Comanche territory.

It was two days out of Fort Smith that Bear ran into Comanches. There had been rain and the country was so vast there was no question about tracking the Rebels. He knew the smartest thing to do was ask the Comanches who had passed through their land.

A hunting party encountered him by a small ox bow lake. The Comanche warriors were not polite.

"You are in our land. Are you enemy or friend?" asked the head warrior.

"I am seeking the camp of your chief, Iron Shirt," Bear said, facing four mounted Comanches. "I have gifts for him."

"Who are you to ride free in our land?"

"I am the Itaxsca," Bear said.

"You cannot be," said the lead warrior. "He is dead."

"The reputation of Itaxsca has come south I can see. I am his grandson and I carry his medicine."

The four looked nervous. "You are a witch!" said one.

"No, just a hunter like yourselves."

The Comanche braves twitched and looked from side to side at each other.

"Two days ride southwest," said one. "He is camped by the Red River."

"Thank you," said Bear. He then took out a sack of jerky and handed it to the lead warrior. "Mitakuye Oyasin."

"Mitakuye Oyasin," the warrior replied.

There was no talk of trade with these warriors. They turned their horses and rode away.

Bear got out his pan and filled it with water from the ox bow lake and put it on the fire to boil. It was the only water around and he did not want to get sick.

Two more days of travel brought him to the edge of the village of Iron Shirt. They did not seem surprised at his arrival. He was met by more braves wanting to know what the Itaxsca was doing at their village.

"I am hunting," said Bear. "And I would like permission to hunt in these lands. I would like to speak with Iron shirt." The warriors turned back to the village.

After a while two warriors returned and said, "Iron Shirt will speak with you. You have gifts?"

He gestured to the two horses he had brought from Fort Smith. He signed for the braves to take them. "They are a gift from the Itaxsca to the great Chief Iron Shirt," said Bear. "I would not come empty handed."

Bear knew that if he wanted information, a gesture of respect was necessary. He rode behind the two warriors who led him to the largest tipi as all the Comanche women stared at him. He felt like a star that had fallen in a foreign land.

The flap of the tipi was pulled back and he was escorted in. Iron Shirt, a very ancient Comanche, sat with his back propped up against a pillow of buffalo hide.

"Cho da Cha," Iron Shirt said in perfect Crow.

"Cho da cha," replied Bear. "You honor me great

chief."

"We have heard of the great Itaxsca in our land," he replied. "You honor us with your visit."

"May I sit?" asked Bear. Iron shirt gestured for him to do so.

"I come seeking information about travelers in your land," said Bear. "White men, four of them together."

"You hunt these men?" Iron shirt asked.

"They have committed the grave disrespect of murder," said Bear. "It is right that they be brought back to Fort Smith for trial."

"Ahh, those that killed Crispin," said the chief.

Bear was amazed that a Comanche chief would know the news.

"Those are a pair of fine horses you brought me," said the chief. "Shall we smoke?"

"By all means," said Bear. "The ancestors may bring us favors."

As one of Iron Shirt's elderly wives hustled about for the pipe. Bear looked around him. Iron Shirt had several scalps hanging in the tipi, they looked Arapaho. There were some dream catchers and a large Spanish breast plate that hung from the lodge pole. He had four wives that Bear could see and many sons and daughters. The pipe came and before it was lit Iron shirt made the sign of the Comanche, a wiggling snake. When the pipe came to him, Bear did the same. Iron Shirt looked pleased.

After the pipe ceremony was done Iron shirt leaned back and said, "The men you want are holed up in a cabin, south of Red Mesa. They came through a week ago, riding hard. It was as far as they could go without food and water. Good game, good water there. Hope they are still there."

Bear smiled, nodded a brief bow to Iron Shirt. 'This is a great bacheeitche (chieftan),' he thought.

"I shall be on my way then."

"Would you like to enjoy one of my daughters before you go?" Iron shirt offered.

"No thank you," said Bear. "It tempts me, but I must find the cabin south of Red Mesa. It is a question of revenge."

"I can see it is a fair trade, this information I give you," said Iron Shirt.

"More than fair, great chief," said Bear. He got up and moved cautiously to the tipi flap.

"Go slow my Crow hunter," said Iron Shirt with a smile.

Iron Shirt's daughters were out in front of the tipi

waiting to be given as a gift to this hunter. They were beautiful, as Comanche women often are, but he dared not push his favors here. Their brothers might like a Crow scalp just to hang from their lodge pole. He mounted Horse and rode slowly out of the village. It had gone well, and he had guessed right about the trade for information.

He had been treated well by Chief Iron Shirt, but he was not so sure about some of the Comanche warriors. He rode slowly and humbly out of the village with angry eyes following him all the way. He knew he was a Crow and that brand of Native was not too popular in these parts. Tribal rivalry was often hot among Native People.

IV

Bear found a place to ford across the Red River. It was brown and muddy because of rain up country, but the snow level had come down over night. He had a feeling that he was being followed ever since he left the village. "What could one of those warriors want?" he thought. The scalp of the Itaxsca would look good on his saddle bow but it would cost too dear.

He pulled off the trail and put Horse to rein. He

backed into the brush till he had a large stone wall at his back and he was well covered. He waited. Dog growled low in his throat.

Soon a horse appeared on the trail. It was a young woman. Bear recognized her as one of Iron Shirt's daughters. She went on down the trail. He waited for a time then got back on horse. He would find out why this Comanche woman followed him. He followed her until they came to a desert patch. She appeared as a black dot in the sand until he caught up with her.

Bear put his fingers in his mouth a let out a whistle. It was so loud it echoed even on the flat desert. The girl stopped in her tracks and turned quickly around.

Bear eased Horse along the trail and walked him slowly toward the waiting girl. As he approached he called out, "Why have you been tracking me?"

She was a girl indeed. She looked barely eighteen summers, slim, and well built, her skin as soft and milky as a baby's.

"My name is Star Shine," she said. "I wanted to know why you did not want any of us, the daughters of Iron Shirt." She seemed highly offended.

"My apologies," said Bear. "But I am on the hunt; my

mind must be clear."

"Oh," she said in a disappointed voice. "Well, do you know where you are going?"

"Iron Shirt said Red Mesa," replied Bear.

"The cabin my father was speaking about is over there," she said, pointing due south.

Bear smiled at her. "Are you going to be my guide in this perilous country?"

"If you ask," she replied.

"O.k." Bear said with a smile. "But I don't want any of your brothers hunting my hair because you're with me."

"Are you afraid?" she retorted.

"Yes," said Bear. "I've heard that Comanche warriors are fierce, not to mention the women."

Star Shine smiled. "Perhaps we'll grow on each other."

Bear was silent and turned Horse south the way she had pointed. Star Shine followed right behind.

By the end of the day they were off the sandy desert and were approaching a high woodland. It was marked by the abrupt beginning of lodge pole pines and a crowded woodland. Things changed in this southern land sometimes abruptly and with no reason. Soon they came to a running stream, the sun just westering behind Red Mesa.

"Time to camp," said Bear. He found a small flat spot among the trees. He made a fire ring with some stones, dug a hole in the middle and started the tiniest of fires. There was no smoke to be seen. He figured they were at least five miles from the cabin.

Star Shine looked on amused while Bear made camp. She was digging the soft dirt with her toes.

"Where do I sleep?" she asked.

"Anywhere you want," said Bear.

"How about with you?" she asked.

"Well, if you can fit two in a hammock," he said.

His gear consisted of a net hammock he strung between two trees to keep the critters out of his bedroll. Dog was already on the hunt and soon he came walking into camp carrying a huge jack rabbit. He laid it at Bear's feet.

"We eat good tonight," said Bear. He skinned the rabbit and cut it up in pieces that he put on sticks over the fire.

Star Shine went to the stream and came back with a skirt full of water cress and Berries. She put them down and said, "No good eating just rabbit. It'll dry you out inside."

Bear smiled, he could see that she knew the trail and how to survive.

The fire was low, and Bear climbed into his hammock, pulling a blanket over him.

Star Shine rolled herself in a blanket down below the hammock on the ground.

"You can come down here," she whispered. Bear didn't reply. Soon Star Shine heaved a sigh of disgust and dropped off to sleep nuzzled by Dog. He liked the Comanche maiden. She was warm and smelled good to him.

Bear awoke to the gentle bubbling of the stream and the faint humming of Star Shine. She was naked in the stream, washing off the trail dust.

Bear slid out of his hammock and saw she had already fried up quail eggs and some of the rabbit from last night in a small pan.

"Aren't your brothers concerned about your whereabouts?" asked Bear. She was startled and jumped. She stood there naked as the day she was born.

"Do you like what you see?" she said softly.

"Put your clothes on," said Bear. "And yes, you are beautiful, but we have no time for play. I told you," he said.

"This is a serious hunt and I don't want my scalp on your brothers' lodge pole."

"Damn!" she swore under her breath.

"Where'd you get the eggs?" Bear asked.

"Oh, I was poking around up stream and ran across a nest," she replied.

"Good breakfast," Bear said. "Did you eat?"

"Yeah," she replied. "And I got dinner too." She reached down and lifted a string of fish. She had five nice sized trout on a willow stick.

Bear shook his head. "Better get dressed. We're gonna be at that cabin about midmorning."

Star Shine wriggled into her dress and moccasins.

'She is quite beautiful,' Bear thought, but he was cautious about beautiful Native women, especially ones not of his tribe.

They were packed up and on the trail by the time the arc of the sun crept over the hills. The dry air seemed still; the day began to heat up. You could hear the clomp of the horses' hooves for miles. A small breeze started to blow and sighed faintly through the pines and aspens. Bear could smell smoke on the wind. They were near the cabin.

"Can you shoot?" he asked Star Shine.

"A little," she said mockingly.

"Take the rifle. You've got ten shots," Bear said. "It's heavy, a .45 – 70.
Watch your shoulder."

The stream ran across the flat, and a snug little cabin lay beyond the stream. They walked the horses slowly into the clearing before the cabin.

Four horses saddled and ready for travel were tied up to the front rail.

"You in the cabin!" Bear shouted. "You are wanted for the murder of Judge Crispin. Come out with your hands up."

The reply was what he'd expected. A sharp crack of a fire arm and a bullet buzzed past Bear's ear, the sound of an angry Bee.

"I don't want you dead!" said Bear. "Put your guns down."

"We're not movin' till Sibley's men come fer us," a voice shouted. "You better git yourself. They'll be here anytime and nail your hide to the wall."

"They're not here now and I am!" shouted Bear. "Come out now! You gotta stand trial at Fort smith." Suddenly there was a sharp report from behind Bear and a scream of pain from inside the cabin. Star Shine had taken advantage of the conversation and shot at a shadow she'd seen at the window.

There was some scattered shooting and then the rumble of hooves. Twenty Grey uniformed riders flooded into the clearing. They all bore the insignia of Sibley's southern command - Confederates.

We gotta go," Bear said. "And fast."

He and Star Shine rode back up the trail leaving nothing but dust. They were pursued for a mile or so then the Confederates backed off.

"They had us," said Bear. "Why did they back off?"

The answer was plain to see. It seemed Star Shine had been missed by her brothers and twenty straight backed Comanche warriors were atop the ridge looking for a fight.

"Now we're in real trouble." said Bear.

"That's our rescue party," said Star Shine. "That's my brother Medicine Hat."

"Oh Lord," replied Bear.

V

"*Hag Mariawe*! (Welcome my friends)" shouted Star Shine. "Medicine Hat, down here!"

Bear was looking at the angry eyes of twenty Comanches.

"Sister, what are you doing with this Crow?"

Bear doubted if he could shoot his way out of this one.

"He is my *haits* (friend), nothing more," said Star Shine.

The bristling Comanche rode down the trail slowly, the other nineteen warriors had their arrows knocked and ready.

"You are with him, why?"

"He would not make love to me Brother," she said angrily. "So I followed him hoping to persuade him."

"This?" questioned Medicine hat.

"This is the Itaxsca's grandson," she said, her chin sticking out in defiance.

Medicine Hat stopped dead in his tracks. "The Itaxsca is dead."

"And I am his grandson, Comanche," said Bear. He was getting a little angry at this warrior spitting on his name. "I go this way from advice by your father, Iron Shirt. She showed up to tag along."

Medicine Hat looked hard at Bear and Bear returned the stare.

"You are such children," said Star Shine. "He has not touched me. You can check if you want."

She made to pull her dress up and Medicine Hat waved her away. "You are Comanche; you cannot lie to me Sister."

"I see you have Greys on your tail," said Medicine Hat.

"They guard the four men I am after," Bear showed his badge. The 96994 shone out.

"I see you have authority," said Medicine Hat. "What did they do?"

"They murdered Judge W. T. Crispin at Fort Smith," replied Bear.

"Judge Crispin always let the Comanche be," Medicine Hat said thoughtfully. "Sister you need to get back to the village."

"I'm not going anywhere brother," she said in a saucy tone. "Not just because you tell me to."

You could see his eyes narrow. He was weighing his options.

"Today we will fight for this Crow," Medicine Hat said

"I will ride too," said Star Shine. Her brother turned his back and motioned for the other nineteen warriors to come. He signaled two to immediately ride off in the direction of the cabin to see what they could see.

"They will see what we're up against," said Medicine Hat.

"I want the four men alive," said Bear firmly. Medicine Hat just smiled a wicked smile.

Bear and the Comanches started working their way back to the cabin. When they were within sight they saw twenty or more horses tied outside with a Grey coated guard on duty.

"Many nice horses," Medicine Hat said. "How about we steal some of them?" He motioned to three of his braves and they slid quietly from their saddles and crept up the creek and behind the horses. The guard was completely unaware of their presence until he was sprouting three manche arrows.

Bear rode up in plain sight and yelled out, "You have four men in there! They are fugitives of the law. They are wanted for the murder of Judge W. T. Crispin!"

Once again, he was answered by gunfire.

Bear could see the distance was too far for his pistols, so he disarmed and grabbed his 45-70 from Star Shine.

The smoke and noise was like his memory of the war. He pulled Star Shine down behind a berm on the far side of the creek and fired.

The Comanches spread in a half circle and peppered the cabin until a white flag of truce appeared out the window. Bear held up his hand and waved at the braves to stop, but plainly it was Medicine Hat who shouted out a strong "Hai" to get the braves quiet again.

"We have wounded!" shouted a voice from the cabin. "We will surrender the four if you will let us ride away."

"Too late!" shouted Bear. "The Natives got your horses, but we'll let you walk back to Mexico."

There was quiet, then three men were thrust out the open door, hands bound behind their backs.

Bear mounted and rode forward to get them. They looked ragged and worn. "The fourth one is dead," shouted a voice from the cabin. "You got three of em,' now go."

"Three out of four, Brother," Star Shine said to Medicine Hat.

"Hai." He looked angry. "I guess no scalps today, but twelve good horses. It is worth fighting with this Crow."

"Star Shine," said Bear. "Go with your brother. I cannot take a woman. These go to Fort Smith to hang."

Her face was a work in wonder. She was angry, then she cried. "I can't go back, ashamed like this," she sobbed.

Bear looked at her and shook his head.

"Medicine Hat," he asked the warrior. "May I have permission to take your sister, Star Shine to Fort Smith?"

Medicine Hat laughed. "She's a damned good fighter. I don't think that'll be a problem. Just bring her back."

"That's a deal," Bear reached out and shook hands with Medicine Hat.

"To think I let you run around with a Crow," Medicine Hat said and smiled at Star Shine.

The three fugitives were put on horses, their hands tied securely to the saddle horns.

"It's gonna be a long ride," said Bear. They tied a travois on Star Shine's horse and loaded the dead man she shot onto it. Bear bundled the corpse up so the flies wouldn't get to it. They headed north.

VI

"You know the South's gonna rise again," said one of the prisoners to Bear. "We're gonna chase them damned Yankees back to Boston."

Bear turned in the saddle and asked, "What's your name?"

"I'm Forest, Forest Edwards."

"Well Forest," Bear said. "I don't much like the Confederates and time can't turn backwards. I'd just as soon shoot you and bring your carcass back, but then I wouldn't be able to see you hang for shootin' Judge Crispin. That's the thing that's important to me. I don't give a damn 'bout your Confederacy."

The other two, Vincent Fainne and Merriweather Heath were strangely silent. Bear knew they were plotting their escape. It was going to be a long ride.

Star Shine was the rear guard. She rode calmly, the rifle cradled in the crook of her elbow ready for anything.

They reached the desert patch where Bear had first encountered Star Shine. Bear dropped back to have a word with her.

"This is where they will try to make a break for it. When it happens, try not to kill anybody."

"You blood thirsty Crow warrior! Is that what you think of a Comanche woman?"

Bear looked at her and said, "Yes."

It was well into noon. The sand was white and hot. Bear was riding in the rear with Star Shine.

Suddenly the three prisoners made a break for the woody line that bordered the sand. Bear came alert as the men started, their horses kicking up dust as they struggled for the tree line. They stopped dead in their tracks though when Star Shine put a shot three inches above their heads and yelled, "The next one will be in the back of your head!"

Bear looked over and saw the little Comanche woman standing in her stirrups a rifle to her shoulder.

"Ok, ok," said Forest Edwards. Bear looked hard at them and said, "I figure you should walk a while. Your horses look tired."

"Sir," said Merriweather. "You can't expect us to walk trussed up like pigs for the market."

"No," Bear replied. "I have another idea."

While Star Shine kept her gun on them, Bear undid their hands and tied the rope around their necks. It was a Crow slave halter which was basically a noose for each of them tied to a lead rope.

So they walked, with Bear on Horse in front and Star Shine in back with the rifle.

It was easier that way for Bear and Star Shine to tow the prisoners to the camping spot. It was not far from Star Shine's village.

"You need to get back to your people," said Bear. "Your village is just over the rise from here."

"I know where it's at," she spat.

"I promised your brother I'd bring you back," said Bear gently. "You wouldn't want me to go back on my word."

"Well," she paused. "No, but Bear Itaxsca, I wanted you to make love to me in the worst way."

"I can't be your husband," he said.

"I don't want any husband," she said. "I just don't want to be a virgin anymore."

Bear looked at her as he thought aloud. "There is a small town just north and east of here," he said. "I'm heading the prisoners there. I will telegraph Fort Smith and have them send a prison wagon for these boys. You can come there and wait with me till it arrives."

They mounted their prisoners back on their horses and rode down the trail to Sanford. It was a typical settler's town, out on the prairie, built around a water hole. All they did there was raise cows and produce beef. It was on a small tributary to the Red River and every winter half of it flooded away with the rains. Upon a hill they had built a general store, a saloon, and a livery stable. Everything else was still in the process of growing.

"I don't like White men's houses," said Star Shine. It was the first time Bear had ever heard her speak with fear in her voice.

"The spirits don't come through the wall cracks, Star," Bear said. "And beds are lots better to sleep in than hammocks or brush beds."

The eyes of the town citizens stared as they paraded their prisoners down the street. Bear let his badge and guns show freely. He did not want trouble at this stage. He knew these men might have some sympathizers in the town. They pulled up to a little house next to the rail tracks. He told Star Shine to wait and keep the prisoners covered.

Bear dismounted. He could see Horse was tired and Dog, who had been his silent companion through all of this, sagged at the shoulders.

"I'm going to telegraph the Captain at Fort Smith to send us a prison train," he said to Star Shine. "Then we'll deposit these men in a cell here in town and wait for federal transportation."

Star Shine was visibly nervous being in a place with so many White people. She felt like she was surrounded by enemies and even with a gun, had no weapon to defend herself. The prisoners were jailed; the dead one deposited with the Blacksmith who doubled as the undertaker.

Bear took her to room 11 above the saloon. He heaved a sigh of relief that this job was almost complete.

"That's a bed," Bear said. "The left side is mine; the right side is yours."

Bear pushed a chair under the door, put a stick which he found in a corner, in the window, then put his 36 colt under the pillow and went to sleep.

Star Shine had other ideas though. She wriggled out of her dress until she was naked and slipped into the sheets, pushing her full breasts against Bear's back. But Bear slept soundly. Dog snored softly and snuggled comfortably in the corner.

Early in the morning there came a knocking at the door of room 11. "The federal prison train is here, Mr. Itaxsca," said a faint voice. "And the whole Army came with it."

Bear blinked, forcing himself awake and answered, "The whole damned Army?"

"Yeah," said the voice. "And a guy named Captain Keene is waiting for you downstairs."

"Oh Jesus," Bear swore. "Keene all the way down here? O.K. be out in a bit."

Naked Star Shine smiled and stretched her beautiful body in the sheets.

"What's going on?" she asked sleepily.

"Oh nothing," said Bear. "Just the whole damned Union Army is downstairs."

"Don't look so scared," Bear said. "They aren't here for you or any other Comanche. They are here for those three we brought in; you'd better get dressed."

Captain Jarod Keene sat in the bar eating a huge steak and a plate full of eggs. He looked up as Bear came down the stairs. A smile passed over his face as Bear said, "What'd you do, bring the whole damned regiment?"

"Yeah," said Keene. "I thought a little escort ride would do them good."

"Well we got 'em," said Bear as he sat down.

"You mean you got 'em," corrected Captain Keene.

"Me and half the Comanche nation," said Bear.

"What happened?" asked Keene. Bear related the history of his meeting with Iron Shirt and of Star Shine's pursuit, followed by the appearance of Medicine Hat.

"Good thing too," he continued. "The damned Confederate Army showed up to help their men escape.

Comanches are good fighters," said Bear. "And they snuck in to steal the Confederate's horses. Their army is on foot headed back to Sibley, I imagine."

"They won't find him," laughed Keene. "Sibley surrendered his sword three days ago and his army has faded away to the wind."

Bear laughed and asked Keene "Are you gonna eat all that steak?"

Keene got another plate and a steak for Bear and they sat eating and drinking coffee.

Star Shine came creeping down the stairs looking for Bear. She was looking like a frightened deer, testing the wind for predators.

"Is that your partner?" asked Keene, pointing with his fork toward Star Shine.

"Yep," said Bear. "She plugged the fourth guy, the dead man we brought in. Shot him right through a closed window."

"Come here," said Keene, as he motioned with his hand and pulled out a chair for her to sit.

"Hait," Keene said.

"I speak English," Star Shine said.

"O.K." replied Keene. "Come and sit. Would you like some breakfast?"

Star Shine's eyes got big looking at the steak. Even though she was a chief's daughter she seldom ate that good.

"You are the heroine of this story," said Keene with a smile. "Without you this would've been a lot harder."

Soon Star Shine's steak came, braced by three eggs. She ate like there was no tomorrow.

"What's your plan?" asked Keene of Bear. "Do you want to come with me to Fort Smith? The U.S. owes you a lot."

"Well," said Bear. "I've got a job to do getting her back to her father and brother, then I'll be up to the Fort for the hanging. That's the last part of this adventure."

It was another day before Bear set out for the Comanche village. He cleaned his two 36 colts, took them all apart, got every bit of powder dust off. He cleaned his .44 colt navy the same way. He reamed out his rifle and re-sharpened his knife. Star Shine sat silently and watched all this.

"What's the matter with you?" asked Bear. "You haven't spoken a word since we came to town."

"Oh, I've been thinking," she said.

"What have you been thinking?" asked Bear.

"It seems the world is a much bigger place than I knew," she said. "Even a chief's daughter can't get the things that are here in town. Do you have to take me back to the village?"

"Yes, I am honor bound to do that," said Bear. "But where you go after that is entirely up to you."

"If I'm not mistaken'," Bear continued. "You are also the richest Native woman west of Fort Smith."

"How is that?" Star asked.

"Well, the reward for bringing in those four Confederates was $12,000 Yankee dollars. I'm giving it all to you." Bear reached into his pocket and pulled out a small book. "This says you have a bank account in the bank of El Paso for 12,000 dollars." He smiled.

She took the little book and stuck it in her medicine bag that hung around her neck.

"Now we take you back," he said.

Bear, Horse, Dog, and Star Shine headed out of town. With them were four more horses for Iron Shirt. Bear knew the Chief would be pleased.

They camped along the trail this time, though Star Shine managed to squeeze into Bear's hammock. She said she didn't like to sleep alone. Horse sniffed and snorted about this bur Dog didn't seem to have an opinion.

It was three days of travel and they finally topped the ridge above the Comanche camp.
They had passed several warriors as they were coming in and they were stopped by no one. It seemed they were expected. Bear took Star Shine right to her father's tipi. She slid off her horse, tired from all the riding.

"Iron Shirt!" shouted Bear. "I return your daughter Star Shine."

The flap of the tanned skin tipi came open and Iron Shirt came out, stoic as always, and dressed in his best buck skins.

"She is a great heir of goods," said Bear as he laid the reins of four more horses in his hand. "Thank you for sending her to me. The horses come from the Long Knife captain at Fort Smith in thanks for your daughter who is such a powerful warrior.

Star Shine stood there looking shy standing on one foot and another. "You are a man of your word," Iron Shirt said. "Be safe in your travels."

It was plain Chief Iron Shirt did not want to admit he had not sent Star Shine to him, but four horses and the return of his daughter was a gesture he would not throw cold water on.

"I go back to Fort Smith to watch the three hang," Bear said. "Star Shine shot the fourth one and he has traveled the star path to his father. Thank you again; she is a great warrior."

Iron Shirt smiled a crooked smile but said nothing.

"*Hetche tuelo*, (May you be blessed.)" said Bear.

"*Hetche tuelo*" replied Iron Shirt. He bent and quickly stepped back into his tipi.

Bear had the feeling he'd better get out of there. Things were even, and he was after all a Crow, right in the middle of a Comanche village. Bear rode out proudly and no one followed him. It seemed a hollow way to leave, but he was glad to be in possession of his hair. It had been a great risk using the Comanche in this endeavor, but it was done. Bear headed up the trail to Sanford.

"Bear!" said a soft voice from a patch of brush to his right. "Will I ever see you again?"

It was Star Shine, mounted on her pony, sneaking out for one more word with Bear Itaxsca.

"No Star," he said. "My country is to the north and west."

"Thank you for making me a woman."

Bear smiled and said, "You were already a woman. Now you're a famous woman." He clicked at Horse and rode away from her. She was crying.

There was a tug at Bear's heart strings as he passed Star Shine, but he knew there was one more thing to do in this drama; he headed back to Fort Smith.

VII

In the early morning of August 28, 1867, the streets of Fort Smith were uncrowded, almost lonely. Bear Itaxsca came into town walking Horse and Dog. The room the Army had paid for was still his and he had the key in his vest pocket.

"Good to see you again," said the man at the front desk.

"Thanks," replied Bear. He was tired and longed for a bed to lie down.

"Town's gonna be fillin' up," said the clerk. "We got a hangin' today."

Bear looked at him with distaste, but he knew it was justice being done.

"Yeah. Captain Keene brought 'em in from Sanford in a jail car," the clerk went on. "They kept yellin' out "The South will rise again," and "Long live Dixie. They had a military court and the new territorial Judge also pronounced sentence."

"Who is the new judge?" asked Bear.

"Oh, that'd be his Honorable Merlin Baker," the clerk said. "Come all the way from Washington D.C."

It was plain the clerk was excited about the upcoming event and didn't have a clue who Bear was. That didn't bother him all that much. What he wanted was some sleep.

"Can you see that my horse is stabled?" asked Bear. He put a twenty dollar gold piece down on the desk.

"Sure enough mister," said the clerk. He snatched at the gold piece. "Eh, what's your name?"

"Bear," he responded. "Bear Itaxsca."

The name seemed to ring in the clerk's mind. "You're the one! You're the one as brought 'em in, aren't you?"

Bear just nodded and started up the stairs, his saddle bags over his shoulder, his rifle tucked under his arm.

Dog went in the room first and checked it out, then Bear stumbled toward the bed locking the door after him. It was good not to hear the crickets and night animals for a change. He tipped a chair under the door and secured the windows. He hit the pillow asleep. Two hours later his sleep was interrupted.

"Get up Lazy Bones," said a small squeaky voice. "Get up and listen to me." It was Wakan Win and her fox. She stood in the middle of the room.

Bear shook his head to clear his mind; his medicine bag burned his chest. "What do you want, Mother?" he asked sleepily.

"Be careful about revenge," she said between chews. She'd already been in his saddle bags it seemed and retrieved some jerky for herself.

"It can eat you up," she paused. "And be careful of the new judge. He is not fond of the Native People."

"Thank you, Mother," Bear replied.

She giggled and headed toward the shadow at the far side of the room, and she was gone.

Bear mused, the new judge, it seems, was not overly fond of the Red Race. Bear would go with caution around this man. He went back to sleep.

It was about noon when a knocking came at his door.

"You gonna sleep the day away?" said the familiar voice of Captain Jerod Keene.
They're gonna hang these guys in half an hour."

Bear stumbled out of bed and unlocked the door. "C'mon in," he said. Captain
Keene came in dressed in his U.S. Army parade dress. "You should be there," he said
smiling, "to see them brought to justice."

Bear nodded and pulled on his clothes, checked his guns and whistled at Dog to
come. The words of Wakan Win echoed loudly in his head, "Beware of revenge and the
new Judge Merlin Baker."

They stood at the back of a crowd of people almost in a festive mood with their picnic lunches visiting with their neighbors. Many children were playing hop scotch on the newly paved streets and matrons rustled about in their new spring hats.

Bear could see Judge Merlin Baker as he pronounced sentence. He looked as though he'd eaten something sour as he stood up in the right hand bleacher.

Bear's senses went into high gear; he knew there was something wrong here.

The defendants were marched out, they had their last words, and just as the

hangman pulled the lever, three men at the front of the crowd drew weapons and took
aim at Judge Baker.

"Get down!" shouted Bear at the crowd. In the blink of an eye Bear had drawn and fired his 36's. As the smoke cleared, all three men lay dead in front of Judge Baker. The crowd
screamed and women wept, but Bear stood tall over the would be assassins. The Judge
looked hard at Bear but could say nothing.

"Jesus," cried Keene. "How'd you know?" Bear just looked at him and said, "Bad
medicine in the air."

Bear looked at the gallows and saw the dangling feet of the prisoners he had
captured and suddenly felt sorry that they had to die such a lowly, ignominious death.
The events of the last two weeks swirled through his head as if in a dream. "Bear," said
the voice of Keene. "Bear, it's all clear!"

In a couple of hours, a man came looking for Bear as he and Keene sat in the
hotel bar.

"The judge wants to see you now," the man said. Keene and Bear followed him
across the way to the courthouse. Bear was keenly aware that the picnickers were all
gone and all that remained were the three men hanging from the gallows. He and

Keene strode past the grisly scene to the court house, up the stairs and through the
main doors. Keene made a motion for him to go in. Bear hesitated, remembering
Wakan Win's warning. He went through the door and faced the Honorable Merlin Baker
sitting behind the dais in the big chair.

"That was good, quick work you did today," the Judge said. "You saved my life
and probably many others. How did you know there were assassins in the audience?"

"I didn't know," answered Bear. "I just felt something wasn't right."

"Hmm," replied the judge. "I had thought of reversing your license to hunt
men," the Judge said. "But on second thought, I now know we need men such as you.
I will add a federal marshalship to it. You are just the tool I need for these times.

Bear could not bring himself to thank this man. He looked too much like a huge
spider, waiting behind his desk, waiting to trap and kill its prey.

Bear nodded, turned, and left. There was an empty feeling in the pit of his
stomach and he felt almost dirty for saving that man's life. He badly needed to go
home. He thought about Keene. Bear had played the game and had moved up to be a
marshal. He thought about himself and Helen. In his mind he heard the noise of gun shots

in his ears. Justice seemed hollow as he looked at all he'd done.

He turned his back on Fort Smith and left – Bear, Horse and Dog. Bear needed
the wilderness to leach out the bad feeling he had. It was 3:25 p.m. He started for
home, knowing it was a long trail.

VIII

It was nine days after he left Fort Smith that Bear once more saw the smoke
rising from chimneys in the town of Durango. It was an hour before dawn and the east
was just blushing a rosy red with the sunrise. Bear felt a great weight lifting from his
shoulders.

Horse felt at home and Dog was full of excitement as they went toward the
Silver Dollar Saloon.

Bear stopped at the hitching post and removed the saddle from Horse's back.
The lantern light shone through the double doors, making a welcoming glow. He could
hear two women singing in the early morning light. It was Helen and his mother
Marsilla. He stood still at the doorway and watched them. The two women were knit in

Friendship. It made his heart feel good.

As he pushed through the double doors he said to them simply, "I am back."

The Reckoning

Tatum Forester was an evil man. He was filled with hate and viciousness as no other man was. He was an officer in the Confederate Army, the son of a bigoted slave owner, who, even as his father had done before him, could not stand the presence of a colored man who was not in chains. Tatum was thin, about five foot eleven inches tall, and bore himself straight backed. He always had an ugly sneer on his face. He was willing to deal out justice for the crime of being colored - cruelly and without mercy.

He was followed by men like himself, Confederates. They were dirty and surly men who could not accept the fall of the Confederacy. They thought of themselves as bad and would do anything for a dollar - Yankee gold they called it.

Thomas Pickering, not too bright but very big, weighed 220 pounds and stood six foot four inches. Thomas was known for his evil deeds for pay - nothing more than a five dollar gold piece would move him to action. His teeth were black and rotten, and he chewed plug tobacco with a vengeance. The other three men, Vance, W.G., and Paul Jensen were likewise ragged and dirty.

"What's the angle for this job f?" asked Thomas.

"We're gonna steal us a couple of kids," stated Tatum flatly.

"Are they rich or something?" asked Thomas.

"No. They belong to someone who rightly deserves our revenge for what he did to us in the war," said Tatum. "Someone you all know."

"We haven't a clue," replied W.G. "You'd better fill us in."

"Who was the leader of those Cavalry jerks that rode us to ruin in the Wilderness Battle?"

"You mean that Injun?" asked Vance. "Was his name Bear?"

"Yup. That's him," said Tatum slowly. "Bear Itaxsca." Tatum considered an Injun the same as a black man.

"He's living with a white woman down Durango way," Tatum continued. "She and her two kids love him. They are sorely color blind. I know he will not refuse to come to a reckoning for them!"

"How do you know so much?" asked Thomas.

"I keep an eye on my enemies." Tatum smiled with a wicked sneer. It was then he pointed to the long scar down the full length of his bearded face that made him look like evil incarnate. His light blue eyes showed such disgust and venom that he could have been mistaken for the old one, Lucifer.

Tatum looked at Thomas. "We ride south to Durango," he said, like a man who had already laid his plans well.

Tatum Forester had become the prime example of the southern plantation owners of the defeated South. He was bitter and prideful, not ever wanting to admit the fall of the Confederate States of America. To his mind the only good Yankee was a dead one. But this! This colored upstart of a man had defeated his army, his wonderful , well trained army! Bear Itaxsca had to pay. Every night on the road to Durango Tatum took out his knife and cut himself on his forearm.   A scar for every night he was not avenged on Bear Itaxsca!

It was early in the morning at Helen's farmhouse just ten miles outside of Durango. Eve, Helen's sister, was bustling about the kitchen getting the children, Emma and Charlie, out of bed and ready for school. The warm smell of freshly baked muffins filled the kitchen as Eve hummed a little nonsense tune. She went to the sink and pumped some water into the basin to wash her hands when she glanced out the window and noticed five men riding slowly into the yard from the road.

"A ragged sort," she thought. She wondered quickly where the children were. She snatched at the shot gun that always lay in the corner of the kitchen, checked to see if it was loaded, and went to the front door. As she opened it the men were busy tying up their horses and laughing amongst themselves.

"What do you want?" she said in her steadiest voice. "I have no food for you and town is just ten miles more down the road. You'd best be getting along."

"Now don't be so unsociable," said Tatum. He was already walking up to the porch. As he walked close he grabbed the barrel of the gun Eve was holding and jerked it easily out of her grasp. Bang! It went off and a shot hit the courtyard. He grabbed her wrist and held on to her tightly.

"Get outta here!" she screamed. The men just laughed at her. She was struggling under Tatum's hard grip.

"What we're looking for, " said Tatum in a stern voice. "Is two children."

"Oh no! Not the children!" Eve moaned.

Again there was a loud shot in the courtyard. Paul Jensen, the man holding the horses, let out a great cry.

"Unh! I'm shot!" He shouted. With a thud he fell off of his horse - dead in the courtyard.

Charlie stood outside the entrance to the barn and held his gun pointed at the men. He was only eleven, but he had grabbed the gun, a single shot 22 that they kept in the barn and did his best to defend his Aunt Eve.

"Get that boy!" yelled Tatum to Thomas. Thomas moved quickly and enveloped the boy like a raincloud and knocked the gun from his hands. He backhanded the boy hard, leaving him unconscious

"Damned kid!" Tatum swore.

"No! Not the children!" Eve screamed again. "Leave them alone!"

Tatum pulled her toward him closer and then shoved her into W. G.'s arms.

"Do whatever you want with the bitch!" he said to W.G. He went looking for nine year old Emma.

Emma was sitting on her bed still in her nightgown, when Tatum crashed the door into her room splitting the door jam. She shivered with fright and couldn't move or say a word.

"Get your clothes on!" Tatum commanded. "You're going for a little trip."

Emma could hear her aunt in the kitchen screaming and yelling "No! No!"

Emma had a good idea what was going on. She was smart, and she slipped off the bed to put on some jeans and a thick flannel shirt.

"Leave my Aunt Eve alone! " she said bravely.

"Why sweetie," said Tatum," I can't help my men from dipping their wicks a little when they get the chance. You don't pay a never mind about your Auntie Eve. She will survive."

Tatum grabbed Emma by her hair and led her through the kitchen past Eve. Eve was crying now, her bare bottom showed as she was on the floor on her knees, her head hanging down. She had been raped by W.G. and Thomas and they stood there laughing about it.

Vance, the odd man out, who now held the horses, chimed in from the porch, "You guys are disgusting, taking down an old lady! Ain't you got no honor?"

"None at all!" bragged W.G. as he spat on the porch. "She was pretty good for an old cow."

Vance shook his head and wondered how he got hooked up with such disgusting sons-of-bitches.

"Take the girl and put her on Paul's horse," ordered Tatum. Tie the boy and throw him on the horse with Vance."

"What about the woman?" asked W.G.

"Leave her," answered Tatum. "She can be the one who tells Bear what we did and rouses him to anger so he'll run head on into the trap."

The men laughed again.

Vance was not so sure about all this. He had been in the 15th Virginia when Bear's Yankees chased the Confederates down to New Mexico Territory. He recognized Bear was some sly Injun and Vance suspected Bear would not follow a blind trail.

Tatum scribbled a note for Bear and pinned it to Eve's dress. It read: *I got the kids. If you want 'em back alive I'll be at the caves above Cat Creek Junction. You and me have matters to settle. Yours in haste, Tatum Forester.*

"Hey look what I found!" shouted Thomas. He had a small Indian by the collar. He was an old man and his hair was completely white. He was struggling against Thomas' big frame.

Tatum smiled a wicked smile. "Let him go!" He drew his .44 and shot the Indian in the shoulder. Bang! Then he said to the Injun, " Now get into town and tell Bear Itaxsca that Tatum Forester was here and there is a reckoning due."

The wound was not serious, but it was painful. Paiute Bill swore but said nothing to the kidnappers. He just got up holding his shoulder. They laughed raucously at him as he stumbled onto the porch. He went into the house looking for something to bind his wound.

Paiute Bill was the stable man that helped Eve with the ranch. He was an old Indian doing the best he could apart from his tribe. He was only 5 foot 2 inches tall and had a bad back. He didn't even know how old he was and when asked he would say, "Oh I'm quite of an age."

"Now you all totter back into town Injun" said Tatum as he sat on his horse. Looking close at the situation he felt it was working out perfectly. "Remember, Cat Creek Junction." He laughed and pulled the reins hard to the left causing the horse to whinny in pain.

The ragged group followed him , Thomas Pickering, Vance, W.G. with Emma and Charlie.

As they went along the trail Emma started to cry. She was trying to hold back the tears, but they came all at once. She thought about breaking away on the horse, but she knew she'd only leave Charlie to face these men alone. She couldn't do that. She also knew that Bear would come after them and it wouldn't be pretty. She gritted her teeth and straightened her back. She would get through this.

II

Bear Itaxsca was sitting on the porch of the Silver Dollar Saloon cleaning his guns. The two .36 caliber Colts were on a table in front of him and the .44 was in pieces on a chair beside him. He was scrubbing out the barrels with a small stiff brush. He was happy and humming parts of the

Crow morning song, "*Hai ya mate. Hai ya mate.*" The world seemed at peace and he was its master.

It was then he saw the unsteady figure of Paiute Bill slumped over the back of a horse coming toward him. He was holding his right arm. The horse was walking slowly to the Silver Dollar Saloon.

"Hey Bill!" Bear shouted, "What are you doing out here?"

Bear got up and walked over to the horse. He could see right away that all was not right. Paiute Bill lifted his tired head and said, "The ranch Bear. The ranch! Some men came and roughed up Eve something awful and took the kids. Shot me too!" With that he fell off the horse into Bear's arms.

"Christ !" Bear swore, "What next?" He carried Paiute Bill back to the saloon.

"Helen," he shouted,. "Come and help me!" He heard her footsteps hurrying toward him.

Helen Hardin poked her head out of the double doors and said, "Damn, what now?"

"It's Bill," said Bear. "Looks like he's been shot!"

"Oh God," said Helen. "We'd better find the doctor. He's probably up at the church," said Helen. "Doc Blanchett needs to see him. Get him in here on the big table."

A couple of men were eating breakfast and came out to help Bear. They carried Paiute Bill into the saloon and laid him on the big Faro table. "Lord, he's bleeding bad!" said Gus, one of the men who had come to help .

Gus ran up the street at a furious pace shouting, "Doc, Doc, come quick!"

Within five minutes Doctor Darrel Blanchett poked his head through the double doors of the Silver Dollar Saloon. "Where is he?" he questioned.

Doc Blanchett washed his hands at the saloon sink, put on his glasses and went to look at Bill's wound. He looked grave for a time but as he examined the wound his face became less worried.

"The bullet went right through," he said. "And it looks like it didn't break his shoulder either."

The doctor stitched the wound up and put Bill's arm in a sling. But Bill was still excited to tell Bear what had happened at the ranch.

"Bear, there's a dead man in the front yard at the ranch! Eve was crying when I left, and her dress is all torn. Those four bad men took Emma and Charlie. You gotta get out there pronto!"

"Oh shit," muttered Helen. "Get my horse will you Gus?"

"She's already saddled out in front!" Gus said.

There was an air of panic in everyone and no one was thinking except Bear.

"Hold on, hold on," he said. "Stop and think a minute. Let's not go riding blindly into a trap."

"Get your guns," he continued. "And let's get as many of the townsmen as are willing to be a posse and ride out to the ranch." He added, "Alone is only good for hunting, not for a bushwhack situations like this might be. Think first."

Bear didn't calm the crowd down much, but he did get five others to ride out to the ranch with him, Paiute Bill and Helen.

Bear assembled his newly cleaned guns then went down to the stables. He hoped Horse was there and not running in the field behind the stables. There was a bark and then a whinny. He saw Dog in front of Horse, leading him toward Bear.

"You two can smell trouble, huh?" Bear said as Horse came snuzzling Bear's neck.

Bear swung onto Horse's bare back and rode him to the stable. He retrieved his saddle and blanket. It wasn't long before Horse was fit to travel. They emerged from the stable straight backed and ready for anything.

The posse was forming at the Silver Dollar Saloon. Gus, an Englishman named Winthrop, Craig, Pete Peterson, and last of all, Marsilla, Bear's mother. She had a good .30 x .30, made by Henry. How she had come to own this gun, no on knew.

When Bear approached her she was stone faced. She said in English, "The whole tribe will hunt for stealers of children, or no people at all! I go with you."

Bear knew his mother and that there was nothing he could say to prevent her joining the posse. Her backbone was as stiff as a two by four when her mind was made up.

Helen came out of the saloon dressed for battle. She wore an old hat, a duster and twin .36 caliber colts showing boldly at her hips. She was formidable. The look in her eye was the look of a she-wolf defending her cubs against all comers. She was willing to spend her life in their defense.

"Thanks to all of you for volunteering," stated Helen to the posse. "And remember, listen to Bear. He has more experience than all of us put together."

She swung into her saddle and they thundered out towards Helen's ranch, not knowing the exact situation. They went carefully, saving the animal's backs for the journey.

It was about three o'clock in the afternoon when Bear, Helen, and Marsilla approached the ranch with the posse. Bear held up his had to signal a stop.

"Let me go in first," he said. "Then if I yell, come with your guns out and ready to shoot!"

Bear walked Horse and Dog slowly into the courtyard. The first thing he saw was the dead man Paul, shot right through the heart. He knew the man had died instantly. The man's eyes had the shadowy look of disbelief that the suddenly dead get when it's unexpectedly their time.

He rode Horse around to the barn and whistled to Dog. "Check it out Boy!" Dog then rustled through the front door and was gone for five minutes. Dog emerged and barked once - that meant that it was all clear.

Bear heard sobbing coming from the kitchen. He drew his .44 and cocked it.

"Eve!" he called. "Eve, is that you and are you alone?"

A reply came "Bear?" It was Eve's soft voice. "Is Helen here?"

"She'll be right in," he said. He sat still, understanding Eve did not want him to approach. He whistled to Dog and said, "Go get Helen."

Dog was off like a shot and three minutes later Helen came riding swiftly into the courtyard, guns cocked and ready."

"Dog," said Bear, as he handed him a piece of jerky. "Good work!"

Dog nodded and sat down, taking the compliment. He also took the jerky.

"I think Eve needs you," Bear said to Helen. "No need for guns right now; she's alone."

When Helen walked in through the kitchen door she stopped with a shortened breath, taken aback by Eve's appearance. Eve was lying face down, sobbing endlessly, her dress torn and still flung partly over her back. She was naked from the bottom down, her panties crunched around her knees. Her hair had fallen apart from the proper Gibson she usually kept it in, and her dress hung loosely from her shoulders, barely covering her nakedness.

"My God," cried Helen "What happened?"

"They raped me Sister. They raped me," Eve cried weakly.

Helen stooped to the floor, lifted her sister and cradled Eve in her arms, smoothing her hair and rearranging Eve's dress. She rocked Eve as her sister sobbed as if the world had ended.

Helen spoke in Eve's ear, "Oh Evie, it will be alright."

"No, it's not alright," Eve complained. "They've got the children. There's a note pinned to my back. I don't think those ugly men have hurt them yet; they're okay for now."

Helen saw the note fallen to the side. She pulled if off Eve's tattered dress.

"Cat Creek Junction?" she questioned as she went into the bedroom and pulled a quilt from the bed. She wrapped Eve in it as she shouted, "Bear, come in here!"

"What did you want?" Bear asked as he entered. He kept his eyes from staring at Eve.

"They've raped Eve and left this!" She handed Bear the note.

"Cat Creek Junction," Bear read aloud. "Tatum has done his homework. Cat Creek is a small town over on the Utah border. It's right in the middle of the Rocky Mountains. Above the town are massive caves that the Paiute Indians believe are sacred."

"Why would he be going there?" asked Helen.

"Because there's only one way in and the same way out," he paused. "I'm not familiar with that area, but it seems a perfect place for an ambush."

Bear looked around the kitchen. White walls, dishes done and put away. It had been a peaceful, beautiful place. Everything was in place, but two chairs were knocked about and a pitcher lay broken on the floor. The Rebels had brought evil into the house. He knew he and the posse were going into the mouth of hell for the children and this was the last they would see of comfort and home that had been theirs for a good long while.

"What does your ring tell you?" asked Helen.

"It is strangely silent," answered Bear. "I think we're on our own."

Bear walked out of the kitchen, his boots sounding on the wooden planks of the porch. It was just then the others of the posse rode up Gus, Winthrop, Craig, Peterson and Marsilla Itaxsca, in search of Bear and Helen.

"What's goin' on," inquired Gus.

"An old foe of mine has kidnapped Helen's kids," Bear said. "They raped Eve Lewis, Helen's sister. They are gone, but we know their destination."

The men of the posse relaxed, but not Marsilla. She slid off her horse and went into the house.

"It's a long ways" said Bear. "Our posse is a day late and a dollar short. I don't expect you to go all the way to Utah with me for the kids. Thanks for coming with us this far."

Gus spoke for the group again. "What can we do?"

"Get back to town and live your lives," Bear said. "You can leave the fighting to me."

Bear spoke directly to Gus. "Gus, can you take care of the Silver Dollar if Helen's gone awhile?"

"Sure can, Bear," Gus replied.

The posse turned their horses around back toward Durango. Bear watched as their figures faded away. His tension eased to see them go. It was a long way to Utah. This was not a journey for old men and greenhorns. It was going to be difficult. He knew that Tatum Forester was vicious. In the war he had been Bear's chief enemy. Tatum had led the Fifteenth Virginia Wilderness Regiment, and it was only by luck and hard fighting that they had been defeated. Tatum's father was a Confederate General, his family deep in Southern culture. He was educated and tough. Now Bear knew the country he was headed for was unfamiliar, and Bear was planting himself in the middle of it for a showdown.

He turned back to re-enter the house and came face to face with his mother, Marsilla.

"I want to talk to you," she said to Bear. She sat down purposefully on the porch, her eyes measuring him.

"You can use your ring," she said. "To hamper them and make them tired."

Bear listened. "I saw your grandfather do it to some Sioux," she said. "They had stolen some of our Crow children. He let the ring call spirits to block their trail."

"I don't have his skill," Bear reasoned.

"Think about it," she said flatly." It was more a command than a suggestion. "You do have the power."

Bear was uncertain. He had not felt even a tingle from the ring over this incident. It was unusual, this medicine ring he had inherited from his grandfather, the Itaxsca. He could see his grandfather's tired eyes again, as if in a dream, as the old man had placed the medicine bag around his neck. Bear had been only twelve then and did not understand the power of the ring. It was not until he was well into his twenties and had gone up against the man the Natives called the Samson had he learned of the power the ring held.

Marsilla broke into his thoughts. "You need to go off alone. Call on your grandfather and ask him what to do. I will take care of things here and we will follow you."

III

Bear, Horse and Dog went slowly along the trail. It wasn't hard to find. Tatum had taken no trouble to hide his tracks. Bear trotted a long while deep in thought. He must track Tatum down and rescue the children. As his mother had said, he knew the ring could help him. He resolved to probe the ring's powers at his next campsite.

Six miles down the trail as night gathered round him, he found a suitable campsite and went about making a fire. He loosened the straps on Horse's saddle and sat chewing on some jerky. He pulled the medicine pouch off his neck and retrieved the silver ring.

"I'll pray on it," he said to himself. He began praying, "Oh, Grandfather, I am still using the gift you gave me in the early days of my life. We are in difficulties now. The children are in danger. Show me the way." He held the ring up first to the west, then the north, the east, and the south. He put it on. He was about to take it off thinking he felt nothing, but suddenly there was a blinding flash of light right in front of him. A man stood, naked except for his leather loin cloth, before him. The man stepped toward him. It was his Grandfather, the Itaxsca.

He looked at Bear, then focused on the ring he held, and said, "You called for me, Grandson."

"Yes Grandfather" said Bear. "I have need to use this ring, but I don't know how to enliven it. It seems dead."

"It guards you and guides you," said the Itaxsca. "Ask and it will show you the way." He stretched out his hand and placed it on Bear's shoulder. Then Grandfather Itaxsca turned back into the light surrounding him. Bear watched, mesmerized as his grandfather climbed a pathway into the dazzling light. The circle of light shrank to nothing and was gone.

As Bear looked down at the ring the blue stone was glowing, throbbing with the beat of his heart. He said to the ring absent mindedly, "Which way do I go?" The ring responded by forcing a pale blue ray to the west. Then it went dark.

"It won't do a damn thing if you're already on the right trail," said a woman's voice from beyond the firelight. Bear focused on the voice and soon the small familiar old woman came into view. She was very short, less than five feet tall. A small red fox stood at her feet and wound around her legs, marking scent. The straight leather dress she wore was very old and wrinkled. It was made of tanned Elk hide, tied together at each side with leather thongs. In one hand she held a walking stick. Her bright brown eyes stared at Bear. "The ring ain't for showing off," she stated. "The spirits already know to stand in Tatum's way. Got any more jerky?"

Bear instantly knew this familiar spirit. "Wakan Win," said Bear with a smile. "What brings you to my campfire?"

Bear handed her a large piece of jerky and she chewed on it as she said, "The ring. You are used to it turning all blue and clearing away your enemies. But in this case there are no spirits involved. It is just men confronting men. You will have to solve it yourself like you usually do." She chewed thoughtfully and then said, "What it will do is tell you when there is a trap. But you already know there is one waiting for you. The ring's chore is already done."

As she arose she said, "Now I have things to do, Bear. Thank you for the jerky." She waddled out of the firelight as the fox yipped once and with Wakan Win was gone.

Bear smiled to himself and shook his head. His mind was a lot clearer now. He found two trees that were close together and put up his hammock. As the fire subsided to embers he fell sound asleep.

Just before dawn Bear was in half sleep and the idea came to him that perhaps the ring could show him the caves above Cat Creek Junction. He took it out as he lay in his hammock and put it on his middle finger.

"Give me a vision," he said. "Show me Cat Creek Junction and the caves above." Immediately a blue haze surrounded him. It was as if he were floating above a small town to the west. He felt he was actually there. He saw trails behind the town that led to the vast cave complex behind it. He saw a group of Natives dancing in front of the cave entrances. There were many trails leading out from the cave into the surrounding country. He knew it was the perfect site for an ambush. He smiled as he saw what he was looking for, a lone trail coming from the land beyond the caves. It led around the mountain where there was an entrance at the back of the caves. That would be his route. Tatum would never expect an attack from that direction. He took the ring off and was immediately back in his hammock, ready to begin the long journey to the caves.

He built up the fire, confident that his plan would work to get to Cat Creek Junction and surprise Tatum by coming around to his unprotected back. He found a rabbit lying beside the fire. Dog had killed it for their breakfast. Bear cleaned and skinned it and put it on a stick to roast. It was handy having a companion who could rustle up breakfast.

A gentle wind blew through the low alpine country. The glow of dawn graced the hills of forest and peace seemed over the land.   All was as it should be. Bear smiled at the gurgle of water flowing down the small stream to his left. Down the hill he heard some deer scuttle across the trail. Then he heard another sound, the hurried clomp of horses' hooves. He discerned at least four horses coming from the direction of the ranch he had left.

He stood on the trail with his guns ready for any skullduggery.

"Hello the trail!" he yelled. He could hear the riders round the far turn below the slope where he sat. "Who are you?"

He relaxed in his saddle when he heard the high falsetto call of his mother Marsilla and realized his people had caught up to him.

They rode in to view - Marsilla, then Helen, Eve, and Paiute Bill. Paiute Bill's left arm was still in a sling, but he held his gun in his right hand, which was still useable. Marsilla rode in her buckskins; Helen and Eve had long brown dusters on.

Marsilla stated bluntly, "We told you we'd be followin' you."

"But Eve..." Bear started.

Marsilla continued, her voice firm, "Eve's decided she's not that hurt after all. Said it's her job to get them kids back!"

Bear didn't argue. He thought how typical it was for his mother, once a task had been set she took charge and got it done.

"Come tether your horses," Bear invited. "Sit with me around the fire." He turned to Paiute Bill and said, "What are you doin' here. You should be in bed?"

"Naw," Bill answered. "It wasn't as bad a wound as all that. The Doc sewed me up good, bandaged it and I rode out. I strapped my gear to the right so's I can still shoot." Bill continued, "This is my country we're goin' into. It's Paiute territory and I know I can help you a lot."

Bear nodded assent. "Well, that is a help."

Helen dismounted and came over to kiss Bear on the cheek. She sat down beside him.

Bear was still amazed that Eve was with them. He said, "Eve! Are you sure you're fit for this journey?"

"Marsilla told me a little story," Eve replied. It made me think...that's some tough woman you've got for a mother!"

Bear realized that he knew half as much about his mother than he thought he did. He asked Marsilla softly, "What story did you tell her?"

Marsilla was silent. Her eyes looked down and she would not speak.

"I'll tell it," said Helen as she touched Marsilla on the hand.

"Your mother, Bear, was violated by some Sioux warriors when she was only twelve. She had just had her first moon time; it was a great disgrace to be a Crow girl and to have been used that way. She was kidnapped and taken, and they used her without mercy. She bided her time and escaped. When she ran away she encountered a Crow boy. His name was Blue Knife. Together they hunted down and killed all the

Sioux warriors that had violated her. She married Blue Knife, who became your father. She is a brave woman."

Marsilla's eyes met Bear's. it was not right to talk of that kind of shame with your children. Silence was the best and only thing she could do.

Bear nodded. "She is a brave woman," he said. "You are all brave warriors. We will get the children back."

Bear tried to imagine a warrior powerful enough to kidnap his mother. Even when she was only twelve it would have been like ripping the heart out of the Crow nation. She was a powerful personality with an iron will. He found it strange that no one in their family tipi spoke of the kidnapping in her childhood. When he looked at her, her dark brown eyes were like stone. He realized there was much more to his mother than he realized.

Eve suddenly spoke. "It's no good sitting and crying about what happened. It's more important to do something about it."

Bear recalled what his Captain Morgan in the war used to say, "Hell hath no fury like a woman scorned." Here there were several women who had been scorned. Tatum Forester beware!

Bear pulled Paiute Bill aside and said, "We need to talk." He led Bill over to a sandy spot and they sat down on some large rocks. Bear snatched up a twig from a dry tree, bent down and drew in the sand.

"Okay, Bill," he said. "Here is Cat Creek Junction, and up this way are the caves. How do you get to the caves from the back. Round this way?" He pointed to the drawing.

Bill scratched his head. "You would want to go round the back. Let me use that stick." Bill bent over the drawing, made a circle to the back of the caves. "There's a small trail we used to use on the right side of the caves. It is really an old hollowed out mesa with rolling hills in front and in back. If we go around and back we will hit the trail on the right side that goes over to the ceremonial floor."

"And this is the main trail?" Bear asked pointing at the way from Cat Creek Junction.

"Yep," replied Bill.

"Okay," sighed Bear. We've got enough of a plan to start. Let's get this posse on the road."

The horses were fidgety and snorted a great deal. They were not used to grouping together in this kind of herd. They sensed that all was not right, but they went along with it. If their riders were calm, then they were willing to bear them to the ends of the earth. But if their people became restless it made the horses unsure about the trail. Bear led the way with Horse. They thundered into the west in search of the two children they had lost.

Bear still wondered if his posse of three women and an old man were up to this. He looked at their eyes to get a glimpse of their resolve. Marsilla still held to that cold hard look of a woman on a mission to hell. Helen, he knew was capable of anything as she went for her children. She was stalwart and as vengeful as a mother wolf defending her cubs. And there was Eve. Eve was out to prove that, even though she had been ravaged, she would even the score as well as a man. Paiute Bill was old, but his face was stoic and unreadable. Bear knew Bill's dark brown eyes were the mask and shield for many things done and undone in his life, but his age did not stop his determination for the task ahead.

The one thing that worried Bear was each person's skill with firearms. Helen had it surely and Marsilla, but Eve had been keeping house for twenty years. She seemingly would hardly have enough skill to hit the target and that could get her killed. He said to her, "Eve, do you know how to shoot a gun?"

"I believe so," she replied with a firm voice.

"Next time we stop to camp, please show me," said Bear. "We've got seventy-five miles or so before we get to Cat Creek, another ten or twelve to get to the trail we need. You will have time to shoot a few rounds off at each camp."

They traveled some ten to fifteen miles down the trail. Bear glimpsed a long flat spot to the side of the road. Many trees were growing there, mostly aspens, spreading a dense blanket of foliage to the right and left of the trail. The place had been a campground before them. Hoof prints were visible in the soft ground and a wisp of smoke still came from a small campfire to the left. There was a small blanket of butter cups growing profusely on the ground, and new grass grew in patches beyond.

"This is the place for the night," Bear said as he pulled Horse to a stop.

All the horses rushed into the grassy little clearing at once like a shot out of a cannon barrel, the rush to get off the trail, even for a short while. The resting place made the crew relieved and happy.

After the campfire burned down and rations had been shared, Bear singled out Eve for a lesson in firing her weapon. She had a gun that had belonged to Helen's deceased husband. It had been hanging on the wall at the ranch and hadn't been fired for years.

Bear said, "Let me see it," and indicated that Eve follow him a short distance and sit down and watch him. He sat on a small blanket and took the gun apart. He had a small brush and oil kit and when he had brushed out the cylinder and the barrel, he oiled all the springs and mechanisms. When he was done – voila,' he had what looked like a brand new Colt .36 cap and ball pistol. He checked out the extra cylinder box and loaded six extra cylinders. Eve was impressed by his thorough actions.

Bear said, "You'll have plenty of ammunition. Now, let's see what you can hit with this thing." He handed Eve the butt end of the gun and said. "See if you can hit that tree, the one in the middle of that stand of three over there."

Eve cocked the hammer, aimed and fired five times. She hit the tree five times.

She smiled slightly at Bear and said, "Daddy taught me and Helen how to shoot when were just little girls. I guess you don't forget even when you haven't done it for a while."

Bear smiled back at her. "I guess you are good to go. But remember," he said. "Shooting at a man is a whole lot different. You've got about half a second to decide to pull the trigger and you'd better be accurate. No second chances."

They returned to the campfire and Paiute Bill was looking nervous. "Hope that shootin' didn't tell them where we are.

Bear looked into the sky. It was turning red with the sun setting in the west. "I reckon they know we're back here on this trail," he replied. "That's how Tatum designed it. It's an old battle trick called "catch a weasel." To catch him we've gotta use bait. For him, the kids are the bait to catch us."

IV

Charlie came to consciousness riding with a man who was holding him tight to the saddle. "He stinks of trail dust," Charlie thought. Then it all came flooding back to his mind, he'd heard Aunt Eve screaming. He had looked out into the yard and there were five men, all dressed in grey. He knew they were up to no good. He had grabbed the .22 and went out to tell them to get away. He had squeezed off a shot by accident and saw one of the men fall from his horse. Then the big man had come down on him like a black cloud and smacked him in the head.

He said to the rider who was holding him, "You don't have to hang on to me so tight."

"You awake now, Boy?" the man said.

Without caution Charlie growled back at the man," Who are you? And what the hell do you want?"

"Oh, we're just goin' fer a little ride," the grisly man said. "We've got your sister too."

Charlie wriggled in the man's arms, pushing down his sudden urge to ride to his sister and rescue her. He began thinking how he could get the two of them out of this bad situation.

"What's your name?" He asked the man he was riding with.

"Vance," the man said curtly. "We've come to even things up with your Injun friend."

"You mean Bear?" asked Charlie. "What did he ever do to you?"

"It's a long story," said Vance. "Goes all the way back to the war."

"What war?" asked Charlie again.

"The war between the states," said Vance. "Your Injun friend road us Southerners to ruin. Now it's time for us to even up the score."

Charlie clammed up and decided to use his eyes and not his mouth.

There were four of them and Emma, his sister, riding in a line headed west. He knew Bear would be following, but he did not know what Bear would do.

The country they were passing through was strange to Charlie. He hadn't been more than fifty miles from the ranch in all his eleven years. The snow covered mountains loomed to his left and right. To him they were not white, but yellow in the westering sun. Under a cloudless sky of blue the line of horses moved slowly through a huge forest of aspens. It was a high level meadow and the green grass seemed to be home to a thousand small rabbits, skittering away in front of them just ahead of the lead horse.

"Time we stopped to rest the horses," said Tatum, who was in the lead. "They won't be on us yet," he said over his shoulder. "They're still organizing." He laughed with an evil guttural sound and his eyes stopped and swept over Charlie, reading him.

"That kid awake?" Tatum said loudly to Vance.

"Yeah," replied Vance. He woke up about an hour ago."

"Put him back with his sister on Paul's horse," Tatum commanded. "Together those two weigh less than a full growed man," he continued. "The animals will last longer that way."

"Okay," said Vance. Then to Charlie he said, "Alright, down you go. Hop on over there where your sister is and ride that horse with her for a while."

Vance seemed to Charlie like an okay character, a more gentle nature than the other three men. Charlie slid silently off Vance's horse, ran to his sister's horse and climbed up back of her.

"They hurt you, Sis?" he said softly near her ear.

"What are you asking me? They didn't do to me what they did to Aunt Eve, so the answer is no they haven't hurt me." Emma spoke softly but there was a hiss in her voice, like she was angry.

"Don't be upset," said Charlie. "I'm studying the situation."

Emma hissed at him again, "The situation is this – we're caught by some evil men and we're going to God knows where, to do God knows what!"

Charlie said firmly, "We have to figure out how to escape."

Emma almost snorted at him. "And to where? We could wind up in worse circumstance if we go wandering away and Bear wouldn't know where to find us. At least with these ugly men," she gestured. Her hand swiped against her leg as if she were wiping off something dirty. "We know that Bear is following us and will come help us."

Charlie's voice was concerned, "But what if they try to do to you like what they did to Eve?"

"If the worst comes, I'll just have to take it," Emma said bitterly. "Just like Aunt Eve!"

Vance spoke firmly to the two of them. "Quiet now, you two, before you get Tatum mad."

Charlie had a brief fantasy of snatching one of the guns from the men and doing away with all four of them, but he knew he wasn't a good enough shot for that. He was biding his time and it was like sitting on a hill of red ants, enduring the torture of their stings.

They stopped on a wide place on the trail still under the cover of the aspens. The men made a campfire to cook food. Charlie didn't realize his hunger was so fierce and he was happy when Thomas came to him and Emma with a couple of tin plates of beans and hardtack.

"Eat up kids," Thomas said with a crooked, wicked smile. "Could be your last meal."

Both of them fell to and fairly inhaled the beans and hardtack. Charlie kept his head down but said under his breath "If I were older I'd shoot that son-of-a-bitch right now."

Emma punched him in the arm and motioned him to shut up. She said. "You already shot one of them. I think you killed him too. Try not to rile that man Tatum."

Tatum lay back with his hands behind his head smoking a small cigar. He was satisfied that he would get one more crack at that damned Injun. His plan was flawless; he would lure him into the cave and trade Bear's life for the two kids. "I know that stupid Injun will do it too," he laughed. "Heroes are always ready to sacrifice themselves for the greater good!"

"Hey, W.G." yelled Tatum. "You got any of that sour mash left? I could use a belt of it!"

W.G. complied with a smile and pulled a small silver flask out of his saddle bags. "Go easy," he said. "That's real fire water." They both laughed as Tatum took a swig.

"Woo Hoo!" Tatum shouted. "You ain't kidding!"

"Make sure them kids are in the middle of the camp when we bed down!" Tatum yelled again. "Don't want to have to beat the brush for them in the morning."

Vance went over to Emma and asked her to move over by the fire. She just nodded while Charlie was defiant and gave him a mean look but complied with Vance's request.

The fire flickered as Emma watched it and her tired eyes grew heavy. She was soon asleep. Charlie tried to remain stiff and on guard, but he too fell deeply asleep shortly after Emma.

Late into the night Emma was jolted awake by a huge dirty hand clamped over her mouth. "Keep quiet!" W.G. whispered roughly. "We're gonna have us some fun." She felt him pull her panties down and he had one leg over her. He was about to lay on top of her when she heard a loud click. W. G. froze.

"You do that to that little girl," Vance said flatly. "And it will be the last thing you do in this world." He stood behind W.G. with his .44 pointed at the back of W.G.'s head. "Doing it to a grown woman is one thing, you pervert, but not to a little girl!"

Emma's heart was thumping so fast she thought she could hear it and it seemed to be jumping out of her chest. In her mind she thanked Mister Vance. She wondered about him, why was he with these ugly men.

"Now get up," Vance continued, right in W.G.'s ear. "Go to the other side of the camp and get to sleep."

W.G. let Emma loose and moved away from her, but only a few feet. Vance growled at him "You stay away from her you fucking pervert, or I'll scatter your brains from here to Utah.

W.G. backed away saying, "Yessir, yessir. You asshole."

Vance said kindly to Emma, "You and Charlie move over here by me. You'll be safe there."

Emma clung to this strange man and protector like glue. Charlie had slept through the whole incident. She didn't know for sure if Vance was a friend, but he was the best thing she had. She would keep him close.

In the dim light of the campfire Emma's eyes darted back and forth between W.G. and Vance. She wondered what she should do if W.G. grabbed her again. Maybe she should be quiet and let W.G. have his way. Maybe he wouldn't kill her. But what if Vance really would shoot W.G.? Would it be her fault? She was shaking a little but stayed close beside

Vance. Warm and bedded down close to him she slowly drifted back to sleep.

Light in the east showed morning was coming in and Emma opened her eyes, knowing the camp was awakening. Someone was seeing to the horses and remaking the fire. She saw Charlie was still in his bed and snoring a little. Mr. Vance was up, sitting on a log and smoking his pipe.

"Good morning, sleepy head," said Vance. "Another day."

She moved out of her bed roll and asked, "Would you take me down to the stream? I need to go to the bathroom."

"Sure Honey," Vance replied. "Shake that brother of yours and he can come too."

She shook Charlie's shoulder and he sat up slowly, heavy eyed and his hair tousled.

"Mr. Vance is taking us down by the stream, Charlie. You behave!"

Charlie screwed up his face at her but went quietly behind them. He was still half asleep and not happy.

About twenty feet from the stream Vance stopped in high grass and said to Emma, "You go ahead and do what you need to. Me and Charlie will stand guard for you." Charlie seemed to relax a little beside him.

Emma knew Vance was being kind to them and wondered again how he got caught up with that bunch of bad men. She wondered if she and Charlie could convince him to let them escape, or somehow use him to stay safe if she and Charlie took off. She would have to think about that carefully.

Emma washed her face in the stream and went into the brush to relieve herself. She was feeling much better as she walked back to Vance and Charlie.

"Where does this stream lead to?" she asked.

"It flows into the bigger Colorado River a long ways down, and then it ends up in the ocean down Mexico way," Vance said. "It's hundreds of miles from here."

When they had taken Emma and Charlie away from the ranch all she had on was her dress and underwear. Her feet were bare and sore, walking on the stony ground. Vance saw how she was walking cautiously. "Hey, I've got some moccasins in my saddle bag. I think they would fit you. When we get back to the horses I want you to put 'em on. Going barefoot out here could hurt you a lot. There's nothing worse than cut feet. Let's get back to camp. My belly is scrapin' my backbone."

Emma and Charlie followed Vance back to his horse. He dug into his saddle bag and pulled out a fine set of Indian Moccasins for Emma.

"I never used them. They're a might small for my feet, but they should fit you," he offered to Emma.

Emma tried them on while Vance and Charlie conjured up some more beans and hard tack for breakfast with one addition. One of the men had shot a couple of rabbits and this was added to the beans. It seemed like a feast after their meager meals.

The moccasins were a little big for Emma, but she stuffed some dry grass down into the toes. After that they fit fine.

"He treats us like kids!" grumbled Charlie to his sister.

"We are kids," she replied. "If you haven't noticed, it's not making him well-liked by the other men."

Emma was going to be ten years old in a few weeks and in another month Charlie was going to be twelve. She wanted to see her tenth birthday and Charlie his. The situation they were in made her thoughtful. It was plain to see that she was the brains of the outfit, but she still could not decide what to do to stay safe.

V

Emma and Charlie mounted their horses and got in line behind the men. Tatum led the men as though he were a general, leading thousands. He was definitely insane. Thomas Pickering was pure bully who had nothing better to do than follow Tatum. W.G. was a sick predator looking for another female to take advantage of. The only one who was seemingly sane was Mr. Vance. The thing that all the men had in common was a hatred for Bear Itaxsca. Emma did not know anything about the war between the states. She had heard it was a big disagreement on whether or not to allow people to have slaves. Apparently, she thought, these men were on the losing side and wanted revenge for their loss. She didn't understand what it was all about, but she knew she and Charlie were kidnapped and were now being used for bait. Charlie was very sullen. He wanted to go down in a blaze of glory protecting his young manhood and his sister, but he knew he wasn't big enough to do it.

"Damn!" Emma heard him swear. "I want to make these men pay!" She watched him closely to be sure he didn't get them both killed.

On they rode slowly down the trail toward Cat Creek Junction. The group stopped at midday next to a road sign that read 'Cat Creek Junction 10 miles.' They were almost there.

The sun was westering, and it was about 4 o'clock as they started down a hill toward a sleepy little town. Emma could see it was nestled right between two mountains with a slight smoky haze covering the town from wood stoves. In the shadow of the mountains she could see lights in some of the house windows. There was a great bustle of people and horses going here and there.

As they came on to the main road a wagon passed them. The wagon wheels creaked, and a smell of old hides and rotten meat exuded from the wagon. The man driving it had a firm scowl on his face and yelled at them.

"Git outta the way!" he said angrily as he passed them.

Pickering yelled back in a sarcastic reply, "Yessir, Boss."

Emma thought it was a dingy little town. There were miners everywhere and the women looked like painted ladies. The women peered at Tatum's group from the windows and shop stoops.

Tatum stopped at the Livery stable to get some oats for the tired horses. He exchanged words with the stable boy, but Emma couldn't hear what was said. Emma and Charlie dismounted and went to sit on a rough plank sidewalk that bordered the stable.

"Let's get the kids something to eat," Vance said to Tatum. "I wouldn't mind some real food too."

"Take 'em over to Betsy's," Tatum replied. "But don't you let them talk to anyone."

Emma and Charlie followed Vance over to a well-lit building. The sign said, "Betsy's Eatery." Both of them sat at the table Vance pointed at. Their legs and feet dangled over the edges on the too-high chairs.

Emma twisted her mouth and said, "Not made for kids."

"Now you heard Tatum," Vance said. "No talkin' to people and we don't want no trouble here in town."

Emma shrugged and said, "O.K." Charlie remained sullen and quiet.

Soon a large woman with an apron spread over her large belly came over to the table carrying a small pad in her right hand and pencil in the other. Her dark hair was greasy, but her eyes were alive with curiosity.

"Hi folks! I'm Betsy. What'll it be?"

"Gimme the biggest steak you got and two extra plates for the kids," Vance said. "And a heap of potatoes and coffee. A couple of milks for the kids."

"That'll be ten dollars," Betsy said. "Say, where you from? You ain't local."

"Naw," said Vance. "We're from Durango way."

"That's a long way for kids to be travelin'," Betsy said. She gave them a suspicious look and raised her eyebrow at Vance, then turned toward the cook in the back and yelled out,

"One big one with taters!" The cook yelled back something unintelligible. Then she smiled at Vance and the kids in a noncommittal way and said, "Comin' right up!"

She navigated her wide hips carefully between tables and took other orders but soon returned with two large glasses of milk for Emma and Charlie.

"Here you go, kids," she said. "What are your names?"

Vance kicked Emma slightly under the table then answered for them. "They're a bit shy," he said. "But this is Emma and that's Charlie."

"Uh huh," said Betsy nodding. "Nice to meet you."

"Yes, Ma'am," responded Emma.

Betsy walked away being called for more orders.

Vance said to Emma, "Good girl, and you too, Charlie.

Soon Betsy brought a huge steak with mounds of friend potatoes to the table. They dug in without talking like they'd been starved for a week. Betsy lingered for a moment, noted their hunger, then moved away.

Charlie got the notion that if he yelled out that they'd been kidnapped that all these strange people would just laugh at him. He was agitated and angry as hell. He wished he could pull a gun out like he'd seen Bear do and shoot his way out. That hope died when he saw Tatum, W.G, and Thomas Pickering push through the restaurant door. They pulled up chairs at Vance's table and sat down.

"How's everyone doin'?" Tatum asked and smiled wickedly at Emma and Charlie.

Betsy was at the table once more, looking strong and substantial. "You be needin' food too?" she said directly to Tatum.

Tatum laughed and drawled out, "Steaks all around, Lady, and coffee if you please."

"Three more big ones," she yelled toward the kitchen.

The clink of cups and glasses and the murmured conversations in the room drove Charlie nuts. How could they be prisoners in this whole crowd of people?

Tatum growled in a low voice at Charlie. "If you're thinking what I think you thinkin', you'd better knock it off or you could get a lot of people, including yourself, dead. This ain't no joke."

Charlie heaved a long sigh and eased up.

About thirty minutes later they were all outside Betsy's place. Night had fallen and Tatum looked around for a place to camp. He settled for a place called The Grove where other travelers had camped before moving down the trail into the Badlands. It was level and a stream ran through which flowed down from the nearby mountain.

"Bed down Gentlemen and Lady," said Tatum. "Tomorrow we go to the caves. That's where we plant our feet."

Emma pulled the scratchy woolen blanket off her horse and wrapped herself in it. It wasn't soft but it was warm. Charlie in his nervousness twisted and turned as he lay beside Vance. He knew that when Bear caught up with them there would be blood, maybe even Charlie's.

It was dark and each person had fallen asleep. Tatum was snoring; W.G. and Thomas seemed to have passed out. There came a rustle and a click of a gun being cocked. Suddenly torches sprang to light all around the camp. Gun bearing people surrounded them. Out of the crowd of twenty people Betsy stepped forward.

"Wake up you scallywags!" she yelled in a frightful tone.

Tatum scrambled to his feet with his weapon drawn. "What's all this?" he demanded.

"I seen you boys with those kids," said Betsy in a firm voice. "It ain't natural. Four men the likes of you and two kids. Explain yourselves."

"Why Madam," drawled Tatum. "How would you ever think something was amiss?"

"We had a telegraph from Durango," she said. "To be lookin' out for two missing kids. I don't abide skullduggery like that!"

"I assure you Ma'am," said Tatum smoothly. "These are my niece and nephew and me and my friends are taking them to see their cousins over in Bolio, Utah."

"That's bullshit!" yelled Betsy.

Quick as a snake, Tatum pulled up his .44 and shot Betsy right between the eyes. Her eyes crossed as she fell to the ground. The smoke and noise of Tatum's men firing deafened Emma. Charlie flattened himself more into the ground. After five of the townspeople's posse were hit the remainder of the people pulled back toward Cat Creek Junction.

Tatum shouted defiantly, "We're leavin'. If you follow us I'll kill every last one of you and burn the town too!"

Emma was horrified at the sight of so much blood. Charlie was retching into the ground. Emma knew Tatum Forester was a madman, but until this moment she hadn't realized how far around the bend he was. He was willing to kill anyone and do anything. He was a terrifying man. She began to be truly afraid for Bear. Would he know what it was he was walking into?

Tatum's men had immediately fired into the posse. Now W.G. just smiled and said as he spat, "Amateurs!"

"Get mounted," yelled Tatum. "We will have to find those caves by night. If we don't disappear I suspect the rest of the town will be down us."

His ruffians performed like the seasoned soldiers they were, and before the smoke from the gunfire had blown away, they were saddled and on their horses, galloping down the trail.

"That was horrible," said Charlie, still clearing his throat. Emma grimaced and shrugged and was silent.

VI

The horses stumbled up the rocky trail in the dark. The rough trail was often difficult to find with so little use. Finally a straight away path led to the caves. It was an old ceremonial site for the Paiute people. Tatum drove the crew until they emerged on a flat open space that stood before the huge maw of the cave complex. The Paiutes had claimed that they could hear the voice of the Creator speak to them in a pure way in this place.

"Home ground!" Tatum said to himself in triumph. "We'll stand here and wait for that filthy Injun. Then we will settle it!"

As they had reached the caves Emma realized again what a dangerous situation they were in. She knew Bear had fought against Tatum in the great war, but she had been just a baby then. She saw now that there were four seasoned warriors willing to kill Bear at any cost. She studied in her mind how she could cut down the odds.

Tatum dictated to the children. "You kids bedroll down just inside the cave." Then to his men he ordered, "Set yourselves at cardinal points for the ambush. If I'm not mistaken, we will be hearing from the mighty warrior soon – so keep low." Tatum looked around the cave. "If you build a fire, make it small and see that it doesn't smoke. We don't want to give away our positions."

Vance took the kids to the mouth of the cave and told them where to put their bedrolls. "Bed down behind those rocks," he said. "There's less chance of you catching a stray bullet."

It was quiet. It was the long silence that precedes the dawn, and Emma lay stiffly awake wondering when Bear would come and what would happen to them all. She imagined different actions she could take that would help Bear overcome these men. "What can I really do?" she asked herself. "I'm not a fighter, and Charlie would blow his foot off if he ever got hold of a gun." Vance had been kind, and yet she knew he would die too if it came to a fight. She lay quietly, almost dreaming. "What can I do to thin Tatum's men?" She remembered then that Vance had told W..G. that if he touched her he'd scatter his brains clear to Utah. "What if I let him touch me?"

The plan grew in her mind as she shaped it. Emma heaved a great sigh and slipped out of her blankets. Like a shadow she moved toward W.G. who was snoring soundly. She knew he didn't expect her to snuggle in and rub against him. He awoke saying, "Little missy, what are you doing here?"

"I'm freezing. I need to get warm. I thought you wanted me near you," Emma whispered.

"You get outta here, girl. I ain't risking my brains getting spread all over the place just to dip my wick into you. Doin' you is hardly worth that."

"Don't matter now," said Emma. She let out the most awful scream, high pitched and piercing.

Vance was stunned awake, gun in hand and full of vengeful rage.

W.G. jumped up with his hands in the air, shouting, "I didn't do nothin'! I didn't do nothin!"

Vance growled at him with seething anger. "Back away from her you filthy son-of-a- bitch! I told you I'd kill you if you laid a hand on her!"

"But I didn't!" W.G.'s voice betrayed him with a squeak. His hands were still in the air.

Tatum came awake instantly to the ruckus. "What's goin' on here?" he demanded. "Ya'll put your damn guns down."

"W.G. tried to molest Emma and I told him if he ever tried it again I'd spread his brains from here to Utah!"

Tatum looked at Emma in the predawn light and laughed. "Vance, she's a clever girl. Can't you see her plan? She's lookin' to trim down the resistance, so to speak."

Tatum turned to Emma and said, "Ok Miss Smartie, go back to your bedroll and let's have no more of this nonsense. It was a good plan, but it has failed, missy." To Vance he said, "Put away your gun. Can't you see when you've been played?"

Vance's eyes narrowed, but he slid his revolver back into its holster. Emma could see now she didn't have a chance. She walked with her head down back to her bedroll. She could see Charlie was so exhausted he'd slept through the whole thing.

Emma could not go back to sleep. She lay there stewing as she watched the light grow and turn into a beautiful golden morning. It was September and the birds were chirping in the trees below the caves. It should have been a day one would be glad to be alive. She crawled out of her bedroll and went behind a large ceremonial rock outside the cave entrance to relieve herself. As she finished she heard a small rustle in the bushes beyond her. As she looked further down the trail she saw the face of old Pawnee Bill. He was holding his finger to his lips signaling her to be quiet. She let herself laugh softly. Bear had come. Now Pawnee Bill motioned to her to come to him. She tip-toed down the incline and threw herself into his arms.

"Now child," he soothed her hair, "you gotta go back and get Charlie. Bear, Auntie Eve, your mom and Marsilla are all here, but you can't see them yet. Go get your brother."

Emma didn't know how to get Charlie up and out of there, but she figured she'd drag him out if she had to.

VII

Bear stretched and yawned, then rolled out of his hammock. The day was yet to dawn as he shook off the night. Helen still purred in sleep and he thought how beautiful she was lying there. He hated to make her roll out and meet the day. Bear checked his guns out of old habit from Army training. "Always check your weapon first thing," Captain Morgan had said. "Just 'cause it was fired yesterday, don't mean it will fire today. I wouldn't want you out there facing Rebs with just your dick in your hand."

Bear chuckled to himself. He missed that crusty and valiant warrior who had ridden for the Blue Coats. He wished again that the Great Spirit had allowed Morgan to live longer.

Bear went down to the small stream that bubbled by their camp. He threw some cold water in his sleepy face. He was leaning over the water when he heard the brush behind him move.

"Getting careless in your old age, aren't you?" said Pawnee Bill. "Lucky for you this damned arm of mine makes me a six-fingered, fumble footed idiot in the brush."

"How's that wound?" asked Bear.

"Not bad. It just aches," Bill replied.

"Before we move on I'll get Marsilla to put some Crow salve on it. It'll deaden the pain for a while."

Pawnee Bill went up stream a ways to get some drinking water. "Holy Jeesus! Look what I found!" He held up a pair of girl's socks. "Found 'em over here on the bank," he said. "I know they're Emma's. It's got that little E she embroidered on the rim."

"Yeah," said Bear. "I could tell someone camped here lately. She's left us this sign." Bear looked around them. "There looks to have been a fight here a couple of nights ago. I hope she didn't pay too dearly for her bravery."

"Shall I go tell Helen?" asked Bill.

"No," answered Bear. "Leave the details till later. She'll be up like a panther and go after them herself if we rile her. She could die an early death that way." Bill shook his head in agreement.

When old Bill and Bear got back to the camp, everyone was awake. A fire had been lit and breakfast was underway.

"Better grab some victuals," Helen said to the two men with a chuckle. "Before the girls eat it all."

Eve was sitting there with a breakfast plate in her hands. The fire of her anger the last two days had burned itself out and she looked lonely and ashamed. Bear saw the tracks of tears on her face.

He caught Marsilla's eye and nodded toward Eve. Marsilla took his clue and went over to Eve. She talked low and gentle to her and in a few minutes life seemed to come back into Eve.

"O.K. soldiers," Bear said to the group. "Bill says there's a way 'round the town of Cat Creek Junction that could put us at the caves before Tatum. I suggest we take it. it will take us past the town on the north side, so let's ride."

The country was hard and the trail indistinct. They lost their way going over a field of large round rocks that hurt the horses' feet. Bear's Horse nuzzled him in complaint, but Bear patted his shoulder and said, "A little further on my friend and I'll let you rest. We gotta get those kids." Horse would go anywhere for Bear, so he buckled down and carefully picked his way through the larger rocks.

They could see the smoke of the small town of Cat Creek Junction to the south, and Bear wished for news, but he felt they might run smack into Tatum there. They came upon a large pan of salt earth. It had been packed deep and hard by the wind, sun and rain. The horses hooves rang hollow on it as they passed.

"Careful how we go," cautioned Pawnee Bill. "When I was young I saw a horse and rider get swallowed up by the salt. It just sucked them both under. It makes a hard crust on top but can be false. You see that dirty colored path over there!" He gestured. "Keep to that darker colored place and we'll be ok."

Soon they were off the salt packed earth and before them was Paiute Mesa. It rose eighteen hundred feet straight up in the air, its sides covered with short bushes, with knots of Madrone and tumbleweed. The sides of the mesa were copper red in the light of the rising sun.

"We're here!" announced Pawnee Bill. "The caves are on the other side of the mesa, and there's a trail to get to them on the left side of the mesa."

"Ok," said Bear. "Check your weapons and let's work our way up there on the trail." He pointed to the slim little track that ran off to the left.

"If you come across any of them, shoot first and ask questions later. And don't forget you've all got knives too. If the opportunity arises, stick them!"

The unlikely band of warriors crept up the trail to the ceremonial caves. The caves were cold and empty. "We beat them here!" said Bear. "Let's let them come, set up their defenses, and let them think all is well. We may be able to spirit the kids away before they know it." Bear found a long stick and drew in the dirt.

"These are the caves," he showed the women. "And this is the bush that surrounds it. Helen and Eve, you get over here, and Bill and I will get over there."

Bear indicated spots outside the circle. "Keep your guns cocked and stay behind cover."

"What about me?" questioned Marsilla.

Bear smiled. "You will find your own way as usual. "You are a much better strategist than I could ever be." She smiled at him and disappeared into the bushes.

It was close to midnight when they heard Tatum Forester's band approach the caves. They had heard the gunfire from the encounter with Betsy's posse much earlier. Bear knew Tatum's group was too skilled at warfare to let anyone take them down.

Somewhere in the darkest hours of night they heard Emma's scream and then the commotion of the men coming to life inside the caves. Bear knew Emma was a bright girl and that she'd played a trick on the camp, but still Bear's group waited, listening. Then as dawn came up, Pawnee Bill saw Emma and knew she was looking for a place to relieve herself. She had seen Pawnee Bill signaling her and she had come right to him. Bill chuckled. She had turned back to the caves then to retrieve her brother.

It was quiet for a time and Pawnee Bill began to worry and think something went wrong. Just as his worry increased, Emma returned, dragging Charlie by his arm with him still half asleep. She drug him into the brush where they became unseen.

The children were rescued!

Pawnee Bill followed and caught up to them on the other side of the brush. "How'd you get Charlie?" he asked.

Emma said, "Oh, those men weren't looking."

Charlie interrupted. "She grabbed me by the ear and told me to shut up and come on!"

"Good thing she did," said Bill. "Now you two get over to the right with your mom and Eve."

Emma ran and this time so did Charlie on his own. Soon they came to the trail that led to the right. They kept running and ran smack into Helen and Eve. The two women had stood listening, but when the kids came pounding, breathless down the trail they whooped and laughed with joy.

"How did you get away?" asked Helen.

"It was good ol' Pawnee Bill," said Emma. "He come and got us. Snuck right up to the ceremonial ground and spirited us away."

It was best that the two children had been rescued, because soon they were missed by Tatum. He howled with rage and could be heard by Bear from a distance.

Tatum screamed at his own men. "You stupid sons-of-bitches! You let the kids get away. Now we have no plan, no leverage!" He screamed again, "You god-damned slackers need to be horse whipped." He had his short whip in his hand and flicked it with meaning.

Vance shouted back at him from the other side of the cave, "We ain't your slaves!"

"Now we got a straight up fight comin' at us, you fool!" Tatum yelled. "Get behind one of these rocks and don't wait. Fire on anything out there that moves!"

Tatum, Thomas, W.G. and Vance knew they were in a tight spot. Without the kids for leverage, even protection from the posse, they were sitting targets with no way out.

Meanwhile Helen and Eve delivered Charlie and Emma back to where the horses were tied.

"You stay here," demanded Helen. "Wait till we deal with those kidnappers. We've got to tell Bear you are no longer in the cave!"

From a hillock just behind the horses a voice said, "Bear already knows." Bear Itaxsca strode into the clearing. "Those scoundrels can sit up there till they rot. The only water they have is a small spring and they will drink that out today."

"We could blast them out," said Pawnee Bill, hoping for revenge.

"Why waste the bullets," said Bear. "They'll come out on their own and we'll be waiting for them."

Bear turned to the children, hugging them both. He questioned them about the gunfire Bear had heard the night before. "Who did Tatum and his men kill?"

Emma answered with her eyes wide. "It was the lady who owned Betsy's Eatery. She came with a group of men from the town to rescue us. Tatum shot 'em down like dogs as they stood there."

"Then you know there will be a posse following Tatum," concluded Bear. "Listen carefully and keep a sharp eye out for riders."

Sure enough, Bear's prediction came true. Before noon more than twenty men rode up and told Bear they were from Cat Creek Junction hunting some outlaw Rebs for murdering the woman Betsy and some of their townspeople.

Bear flashed his Marshall's badge and took charge of organizing the posse.

"Glad to see the law is here," muttered a man named Henry. "Then anything we do is legal. We can hang those ruffians."

"Now, if you can catch them," said Bear. "We'll take them back to Durango for trial. Then you can hang 'em."

The day drug on, one of those still autumn days with no wind and still a warm summer sun beating down on everyone. It grew hot for the men in the caves and the wait was terrible.

Bear stood at the foot of the hill that led up to the caves.

"We got the kids!" He yelled up at Tatum. "You might as well surrender. You don't have enough water and there's a posse from town surrounding you. You don't have a chance of coming out alive unless you surrender,"

"Not this time," yelled Tatum in return. "You ain't gonna win this time!"

A single shot from Tatum rang out in answer and Bear felt the swoosh of wind from a bullet pass too close to his head.

"O.K," Bear shouted to Tatum. "Suit yourself."

Bear turned back to the posse and said, "They're gonna try to find a way out. Watch that trail where the kids escaped. They'll stumble across it sooner or later and try to sneak out of their predicament.

Back with the children, Helen was hugging Emma, but Charlie sat there sullen as if the weight of the world was on his shoulders.

"What's the problem?" Helen asked her son.

"I didn't do a damned thing to help us," he said with a lowered lip.

Helen looked at him, knowing he was right on the edge of puberty, heading toward manhood.

"I don't know if I could have done anything in that situation either, Son," Helen said. "Emma was just in the right place and happened on Pawnee Bill as she came out of the cave."

"Yeah, I know," said Charlie with a long face. "I was just along for the ride."

VIII

Tatum Forester had run out of luck and he knew it. He didn't have the kids as hostages to force a fight so he could gun down the savage Bear that pursued his Rebs. So they were trapped.   He saw the posse from Cat Creek Junction arrive and surround the cave entrance, but they all stayed out of rifle range. The only thing for his band to do was to break out of this miserable trap or die here.

"Get your horses saddled," Tatum commanded his men. "We're getting out of here! That damned Injun has us bottled up just like he did back in Taos. I ain't gonna let him take me like this!"

"Shouldn't we separate, go in different directions?" asked Thomas.

Vance was tired of the whole affair. He responded, "No! if we thunder down on them we just might break out in the land below. A little show of force could work to our advantage."

"He's right!" said Tatum. "Let's charge 'em away from Bear where I can see the posse has thinned out a bit. If we ride at them hard we can break through!"

It was agreed and Tatum's band waited till it was dusk. Then Tatum and his men mounted and pulled together in a loose formation. The sun had dipped to a slant where it was in the eyes of the posse and the timing was perfect.

Tatum, Thomas, W.G. and Vance rode down the hill ready for the final battle. The posse was just fixing to eat dinner. Tatum and his men went through the brush and spurred into a gallop. It looked to Tatum like they were going to make it, all except for Bear.

Bear, Horse, and about ten posse members stood in their way. Again they were surrounded. Tatum was focused on the rush and trying to shoot his way out, but Bear winged him in the arm. Tatum fell from his horse.

Thomas' horse stepped wrong and tripped, sending Thomas flying. Vance stopped and put his hands over his head in surrender, but W.G. managed to keep going. He was just topping the hill behind the mesa when he felt an excruciating pain in his belly. Looking down he saw a long knife sticking in him just below his ribs. Marsilla gave a victory cry and grabbed him by the hair, slit his scalp smoothly and yanked. He could hear his hair leave his head, and blood trickled down his face. Her triumphant scream was the last thing he heard as blackness overtook him and he died.

Marsilla stood over him, panting with rage, his bloody scalp in her right hand.

"You will never rape another woman!" she spat at his withering body. "Never again!"

The battle was over. The Tatum Forester gang, what was left of it, was taken into custody and led back to jail in Cat Creek Junction. The three men were a somber looking lot in their filthy, worn Confederate uniforms. Tatum Forester held his head high though, like he imagined he was in an awards parade. Thomas Pickering in contrast, looked from side to side like a wolf in a trap, waiting for an opportunity to escape. His dirty face was a study in anger and contempt. Vance hung his head in humility seeing WG.'s scalp hung from Marsilla's saddle.

The twenty posse riders along with Bear, Eve, Helen, Marsilla, Paiute Bill and the two children rode behind the Tatum raggedy troopers pushing them on to Cat Creek.

"My cause was a noble one," bragged Tatum loudly. "No jury will convict me of besting a slave!"

Bear smiled silently, but Helen spoke up, "Yet it is the Indian who has you in a pickle." She fairly sneered at Tatum.

The ride to Cat Creek was about ten miles. Soon the crew of kidnappers sat in cells in the jailhouse.

Helen, Bear and the children got two rooms above the Dirty Miner Bar. Eve and Marsilla chose to stay above the stables in a room the livery man had for rent.

Eve talked to Marsilla in a lowered voice. "You actually scalped him," she said. Eve was in awe of Marsilla's courage.

"You betchum," responded Marsilla matter-of-factly. "He raped his way to a fate like that from a woman"

Eve said almost in a whisper, "You were raped too. It was awful and I wanted him punished too, but..."

"But what?" Marsilla responded firmly. "When men like that meet an end like he did, maybe other lustful men will think twice. I have the scalp of every man who raped me, and I will give you this man's if you want it. He got what was coming to him. A reckoning. I could see it in his eyes as he died."

Eve shuddered and said, "That's savage." She looked down at her toes.

"Ain't it though," said Marsilla. "But us Injuns are known for our savagery."

"I would have made him eat dirt or something," Eve offered meekly. "But you murdered him."

Marsilla looked at her with a deep understanding. "He too was a savage," she said. "It was not murder. I stopped a runaway criminal. Those are two different things."

Eve lifted her head and looked straight into Marsilla's eyes. "Thank you. I would not have had the courage to do what you did."

Marsilla's look back to Eve was a hard stare, her eyes like glass beads in her face. "I will leave his scalp here for you," she said. "To give you courage in the future. Now you'll be wanting some sleep."

Marsilla left Eve to her rest silently. Eve had tears in her eyes as she bedded down. It was a cruel world they lived in and she knew it justified a cruel response.

The three prisoners were chained to their bunks in Cat Creek Junction Jail. Bear said they would be moved in the morning. Bear planned on taking them back to Durango, some seventy miles away, and having them tried there.

Some of last night's posse gathered on the porch in front of the jail. Henry, the leader of the posse said, "Why can't we have the trial here? We all loved Betsy and Tatum just shot her down with five others of our tow. They were gunned down like rabid dogs in the street. Those Rebel men had no care for the living!"

One of the other men in the posse said aloud, "You ain't a judge, that's why. We need to make it legal. Just go along with the Marshall."

Henry bit his lip and walked away followed by the riders. Still it did not go down well with most of the posse and the locals. They wanted Bear to allow them to string up Tatum and his two men. It stood to reason that since the Rebs had killed a beloved woman and townspeople that the Cat's Creek citizens should have their way. Durango was too long a way to ride for what seemed to be the obvious outcome.

Paiute Bill had witnessed the discontent flying around the town. He took the news back to Bear that all was not well with the Cat's Creek townspeople.

"They're over at the saloon," he told Bear. "Getting liquored up. They mean to take Tatum and his men out and hang 'em, even if they have to run over you to do it!"

"I've seen things like this before," said Bear. "They'll do one evil to mend their hurt souls and regret it after they sober up. We can't let this happen."

"Bill, you get a shotgun from the cabinet here in the jailhouse and back me when they come. I'll be sittin' right here in front to face them."

"Don't know how good I'll be shooting left-handed," Bill said. "But I guess it don't matter with a shot gun."

Together they planted themselves in front of the jail to wait for the inevitable rush of men who wanted to stretch the necks of Tatum, Thomas, and Vance.

Helen, who stood beside Bear, had mixed feelings. She thought a hanging here was as good as anywhere, especially to appease the locals who had dealt with the Rebs, but she would back her man regardless.

By 9:30 it was full dark and the noise at the Cat Creek Saloon was getting louder and louder.

"The only thing stoppin' us is that Injun," shouted one man "Let's just take them killers anyway. Who's with me?"

Ten men pushed forward and ran out of the saloon, followed by the remainder of the men who were unsure of such a move. They lit torches and marched heavily from the saloon to the jail.

Other townspeople joined them and now there were thirty men in unison as they shouted, "Hang the Rebs!" They were ready for blood and they knew they were in the right. The stomping of their feet made the ground shake. They were sure that justice would be done, except for one thing in their way - Bear Itaxsca.

Bear stood on the jail porch like a bronze statue. He had a shotgun in his hand and his two .36 colts in his sash. He waited until the mob was twenty feet away from him and then spoke.

"You can't have them!" Bear's voice was loud and firm.

"But they murdered Betsy and our townspeople," several shouted. "You even got witnesses!"

"No!" Bear shouted. "You will not take them. I'll shoot the first five of you who try!

Who will it be? You gonna step up to get killed so you can get the killers? Who's gonna be first? You can get me in a rush, but five or more of you will join those others in the cemetery, turning stiff in the morning light. Which ones now? Let's get it over with you brave men!" He paused. "Don't forget the Federal Marshall from Fort Smith will ride you down to a man if you kill me. Let's get it over!"

Pawnee Bill leaned on a chair behind Bear and to the side. He leveled his shotgun at the crowd. Then another click of a gun was heard that Bear did not expect. It was young Charlie. He stood at Bear's right leveling the Greener he'd found on the wall in the jailhouse. He squinted and aimed at the crowd of angry men. He had cocked his weapon and meant business. Bear was glad that Charlie would stand like a man in a terrifying situation.

"Ha!" said Bear. "Make it more like the first fifteen of you that will be feeling the sting of gunshot and growing cold by dawn. Is it worth it?"

Matt Latimer was the first to fold. He lowered his weapon and said, "Those men ain't worth dying for and we can see that you mean what you say. But how can we be sure they will actually hang Tatum's Rebs back in Durango?"

Matt was a husky man with huge muscled arms. He wore a blacksmith's apron and his hands bore the small burn scars one gets from working a forge. He was sober and angry, angry that Betsy was dead, and they had not seen the murderers being punished.

Bear addressed him. "What's your name?"

"Matt," he answered "Matt Latimer. I'm the town blacksmith"

"Well, Mr. Latimer," Bear continued. "These boys will all have their necks stretched when a judge hears the case. We have the best witnesses right here. This young man is Charlie. Charlie did you see the Rebs shoot Miss Betsy down?"

"Yes sir, I sure did." Charlie's knees were shaking but he did not flinch.

Bear continued. "They deserve a noose, but only if a judge says so!"

When the lynch mob heard Charlie's young voice they seemed to lose steam. Slowly the men wandered away from the crowd till it dwindled to not a man in protest. Then Charlie wondered if his words or Bear's, or if the guns that Pawnee Bill, Helen, Bear and Charlie had pointed at the mob had convinced the townsmen to calm down. At any rate, Charlie began to ease up inside himself, realizing he had played the part of a man in standing up with Bear.

"It'll be a sleepless night," Bear said to Pawnee Bill and Charlie. "We'll have to bunk in the jail till tomorrow." He looked at Helen and said, "It will be ok now. You can go back to the hotel. We'll be all right."

In the morning Bear and the two with him woke with stiff arms and backs. Bear muttered under his breath, "If we had let those Rebs hang I could have slept in a bed last night." He went down to the livery and found the blacksmith had just finished work on a wagon with barred cages for transporting the prisoners.

"Looks good," Bear said to Matt Latimer.

"About last night," Matt said. "I apologize for the big ruckus."

"Yeah," Bear responded. "Tempers run high in a situation like that."

Matt handed the keys to Bear with lowered eyes. The wagon was a regular buckboard but fixed up with an iron cage in the back. Benches were along the sides for the prisoners to sit, and an iron door with a heavy lock decorated the back.

The worn wood of the buckboard and the used wheels looked rough, but steady.

Bear nodded to Matt knowing the cage was well made. He and the blacksmith hitched up two horses to the wagon and Bear drove it over to the jail. The night had been frosty, and the early sun had melted the frozen ground into a muddy slush. Bear scraped the mud from his boots growling, "Towns are untidy."

Inside the jailhouse Bear said to the prisoners, "Well boys, are you ready for another journey?"

Tatum glared at him with unbridled hatred, but he kept his mouth shut. Thomas sniveled a little, while Vance with his head lowered seemed to accept his fate.

Bear drew his pistol and pointed it directly at Tatum's head. He pulled the hammer back.

"Put these on," he commanded Tatum. Bear threw a set of shackles into the cell. Once Tatum was trussed up he did the same to Thomas and Vance.

After the Rebs were shackled Bear threw open the jail cell and followed them with his gun in hand as they shuffled out to the wagon.

"Climb in the back," he directed them.

By then his group had assembled: Eve, Helen, Pawnee Bill, Marsilla and Emma and Charlie, all ready to travel. They rode behind the prisoner wagon to see the Rebs delivered to Durango.

As they reached the edge of town, they encountered ten men on horseback, ready to travel with them. One man said, "We come to see that justice is carried out. The town wants its own witnesses."

Ben looked them over. "Don't you drive the stagecoach around here?"

"Yeah," the man said. "Tim's my name," the man responded. "Tim Brantlett."

"How would you feel about driving this wagon?" Bear asked.

"Sure as hell beats riding a horse," Brantlett said.

Bear slipped off the wagon and retrieved Horse. Now Dog was behind Bear and Horse and keeping an eye on everyone. The whole escapade had been hard on Dog. He wasn't used to sharing his master with so many people. Now things were more like they were supposed to be. His ears pricked forward for sounds along the trail. He was happy.

IX

As Bear's group rode along with the prisoners in tow, it was pitiable to hear the three men in the caged wagon discussing how they would escape and where they would go afterward.

In a low voice Tatum said, "They will never try us for getting back at a slave. It ain't civilized."

"We're not in the old South, you idiot," retorted Thomas. "They're gonna hang us if we can't get away."

"It was war!" Tatum said defiantly.

Vance and Thomas shook their shaggy heads. They could see that Tatum had plainly lost his power to reason. It was sad for them to see.

As they neared their original camp site, Bear stretched in the saddle. It had been a long seven days and he was ready for some rest. Helen and Bear pitched the hammock between two aspens and slept the sleep of exhausted travelers.

In the middle of the night there was a small but distinct rustling near the campfire. It was Wakan Win with her familiar, the fox. Marsilla was standing guard, having vowed not to sleep until justice was done, so she sat by the fire stoney-eyed staring into the flames. She was unmoved by Wakan Win's presence.

"What do you here, Spirit woman?" Marsilla said in a flat tone.

"I have come to see my boy," said Wakan Win.

"He is not your boy, Mother," said Marsilla. "He is mine! He sleeps. Do not bother him."

"Grandfather always favored you, my child," said Wakan Win. "It must be to you I speak then."

"Speak then," Marsilla snapped. "And do not waste my time."

Wakan Win spoke very slowly. "All right Daughter. Beware of your vengeful heart. It will ride you to ruin though your face is of stone and your will is of iron. You must let some of your anger go. If you do not, it will eat you from inside like a canker. I have spoken."

Marsilla reached behind her and retrieved a piece of jerky. She handed it to Wakan Win. The old Spirit Woman took it, said thank you, and waddled out of the firelight and was gone.

Marsilla, her face still a stone mask, remembered the stifled screams as each of the Sioux warriors had held her down and took his turn raping her. Her lip sneered and curled as she recalled scalping the last man she had caught up with as he pled for mercy. She felt their blood had never left her hands. She remembered the handsome Crow warrior, Blue Knife, when he found her, learned of her fate and how he had avenged her. He had taken on twenty Sioux warriors and overcome them all.

Marsilla thought about the bitterness she felt in her throat and belly and how Blue Knife had waited a full month before approaching her with deep emotion. He had taken her into his tipi, vowed to protect and care for her. He had been so patient with her until she longed for his embrace. Why couldn't all men be like him, she wondered.

A few tears squeezed from her eyes, the first in many years since Blue Knife's death. She had borne him two sons and he was content with her. She still felt rage in the pit of her stomach for men who took their pleasures wantonly. She could not shake that hatred.

"Are you alright?" whispered Pawnee Bill. His gentle voice startled her from the darkness. "Can I help you?" he asked.

She answered in a clipped tone. "I'm fine." He had intruded on her agony.

"You'd better get back to sleep," Bill said. "It's a couple of hours before dawn. We ain't goin' nowhere till then, and I can watch the camp so you can sleep a bit."

"You are kind to worry about me," she said. "But I'll be fine."

Paiute Bill nodded and went his way, making the rounds of the camp. Marsilla took him at his word and laid down for a badly needed nap.

The camp stirred as the arc of the sun pushed its way over the mountains. Bear and Helen rolled out of their hammock to the sound of the prisoners moaning in contempt. They had spent the night on the hard floor of the wagon.

"Oh," moaned Thomas. "Why don't you just shoot us here, instead of leaving us in this torturous cage you've got us in?"

Tatum crawled up on the bench and his eyes darted back and forth like a rat trapped in a cage.

"We'll be in Durango tonight," said Bear. "You can stretch out then, all of you, when you get into a nice jail cell."

"You need to let 'em out for a spell," said Helen. "They could die in there. We can cover them, and they'll be ok."

"I suppose you're right," agreed Bear. "They can relieve themselves and we can feed them."

"Ok," Bear said as he unlocked the wagon. "File out to get some victuals."

Eve had taken pains to cook up a big breakfast of salt pork, beans and a couple of rabbits. "Wilderness Stew" she called it. it was the best food since they'd been traveling. The prisoners fairly inhaled the hot goodness of it. Tatum surprisingly said, "Good cookin', Ma'am. Wish we could eat like this all the time."

Eve was taken in by his comment and felt pity for the three ragged prisoners, in spite of the ugly deed that had been done to her. "Gotta feed growin' boys," she said.

Bear wondered at her comraderie with the Rebs and realized she would make some man a wife in the future.

Bear was also watching as Emma paid attention to Vance. She brought him his plate of food and talked to him as he ate.

Vance said to her softly, "I never meant you no harm, little lady. I was just part of Tatum's command and I followed his orders"

Emma made no reply, but it was plain to see she reckoned Vance to be a kind man.

Breakfast done, the prisoners shuffled back into the wagon to start the last long haul into Durango.

X

Bear's sweat dripped from his brow as he rode the last few miles to Durango, Colorado. It had been a long and difficult journey trying to make time with the slow moving wagon. With the prisoners' cage it was a heavy load and the horses pulling it heaved heavily with every step.

"Stop for a bit," Bear said. "We're killing the horses in this heat. Let the deputies come from town and take these men in." He pointed toward Tatum, Thomas, and Vance.

"Helen," Bear called to her. "Can you ride into town and get four or five men to help us?"

"You betchum," she said and off she rode at a gallop toward town.

Bear checked his guns as he always did when he had a spare five minutes. They were cap and ball .36 caliber Colts. Their shot was clean and deadly. He had seen a new type of cartridge guns, but he trusted his Colts. They had seen him through many hard times. His .44 Navy was a cartridge type and it seemed clumsy to him.

"Got to change with the times," he said to himself. "When this mission is all done I'll look into a conversion kit for my Colts. It would be handy not to have to change cylinders in the middle of a gunfight.

Just then Helen returned with five men from Durango. She said almost breathlessly, "Joe Bixby, Fred Allen, and these others are with you, Bear."

"Good," said Bear. "Let's get them prisoners out of the wagon and walk them into town."

"Why walk them in?" asked Bixby.

Bear gave a frown and said, "Because this one here, if he could break free, can ride like a Kentucky jockey if you give him a chance. On foot with irons he's manageable. It will be good for them to stretch their legs a bit too. They've been cramped up in there a long time."

The group was quite a sight and resembled a ragged parade. The five townsmen rode three in front and one at each side of the prisoners. Bear and his entourage of three women, one old Indian man, and two kids rode behind, with the witnesses from Cat's Creek Junction following them. The prisoners slogged through the dirt streets of Durango, Colorado and finally came to rest at the steps of the jail.

Bear undid their shackles one by one and escorted them into the jail cells. This would be their last place of rest, if all went right on the side of justice.

Bear and Helen went to their room, number 11 as always, above the Silver Dollar Saloon. Eve, Marsilla and the kids were put up at the boarding house across the street from the Bar.

Bear wanted everyone who'd been involved with the prisoners' capture to be close at hand. He was still anxious and expected trouble until the deed was done, but he had no idea what it was that made him wary.

The summer sun rose hot and shone down on the dry dusty streets of Durango. The cavalcade of men and horses crowded the streets.

Nathan Forester, Tatum's tough and aging father, had come into town with twenty-two hired men with the aim of getting his son out of jail.

Paiute Bill had slept over at the jail and saw the Nathan Forester coming in to town. He locked up the jail and ran to tell Bear. "We got trouble," he said loudly to the locked door of room 11. Bear opened the door a crack and said, "What now?"

"Nathan 'Kiss your hand' Forester has come with his men to get Tatum and the other two men free?"

"Oh crap," Bear said. "I knew something was coming. The judge is due in on the stagecoach later today."

From behind Bear Helen said, "Why don't you send those men down to Mama Red's? She'd enjoy the business and we could tell Forester's men the bill is on the Saloon.

Let's try to kill them with kindness." Bear agreed to her plan. Helen dressed in one of her fancy gowns quickly and rushed out the door beside Bear.

Nate Forester and his men had followed old Paiute Bill to the Saloon.

Helen stood in front of Bear as he stood in the saloon doorway. At first they were greeted by hoots and jeers from Nathan Forester's men.

"I'm here to get my boy," Nathan Forester addressed Helen. "I believe he has been unjustly incarcerated."

Helen spoke up. "Mr. Forester?" Forester tipped his straw-boater hat toward Helen.

"I can see there's been some confusion here," Helen continued. "I would like to invite you and your men to stay down at Mama Red's house without charge, paid for by my Silver Dollar Saloon, and await the arrival of the circuit court judge. He's due in today."

Nathan Forester bowed to her in his saddle. He was a tall, thin man with a short cropped white Van Dyke beard. He was sun tanned and tough looking but counted himself a ladies' man. He was used to commanding his men and one could see his hands were not rough, as though he'd never done a day's labor. He was used to the better things in life. His grey suit was immaculate, and his polished boots shone in the sun.

"I will take your offer kindly," Forester said, appraising her beauty and auburn red hair. "The place at the end of the street then?" he asked.

"Yes, sir." Helen smiled and gave a small curtsy at the same time.

"I am glad to see there is still some manners and hospitality out here in this Western dust," Forester said. He turned his horse toward Mama Red's and his men followed him.

Under her breath Helen said, "Best little whore house this side of Fort Smith." She moved past Bear who shook his head but was pleased with her womanly wisdom.

Bear smiled. "No need for guns with a woman like that," he said.

The judge rolled into town before noon. He was hurried and grumpy, knowing he was late.

"The damned wheel came apart on us in Laredo," he explained to Bear at the courthouse. "Then we had to fight off robbers about fifty miles down yonder," pointing to the Southeast. We're lucky to make it here at all. This damned territory is too big for one circuit judge." He heaved a sigh and asked Bear, "What have you got for me now?"

"Three kidnappers Judge Craig," Bear responded.

Thomas Craig had been appointed circuit judge by the Territorial Authority year before last at Fort Smith. He was a small, serious man with a keen eye for right and wrong. He was balding, kept one pair of glasses on his face and several more in his pockets. He had a small paunch for a stomach that he called his reward for eating well.

"Anything else to it?" the judge asked.

Bear started slowly. "As usual there's a murder involved." Here Bear drew in his breath then continued. "We brought in the Rebel man Tatum and his cohorts; his father is here to make sure everything goes to his son's benefit"

"Great!" Judge Craig said sarcastically. "High adventure in the Rockies!"

Judge Thomas Craig was a fair man but always stuck to the law. He was a hard-faced territorial judge dedicated to bringing law and order to this untamed part of the world. He was shadowed by the four tough deputies that had traveled with him. They were the roughest men Bear had ever encountered. They were territorial guards at the Fort Smith prison, their duty being to protect Judge Thomas Craig. Their presence promised to cause quite a show down with Nathan Forester's men.

By early afternoon Judge Craig had been fed and visited by his favorite lady from Mama Red's, then was ready to hold court. He entered in his robes and court was convened. The prisoners were ushered in. The locals and Forester's twenty-two men crowded into the small courtroom. The heat was stifling.

Judge Craig banged down his gavel twice and stated, "Herein starts the territorial court for the Southwest Territories of the United States of America! First case!"

Bear stepped forward and stated, "The charges are as follows: Kidnapping, rape and murder. They kidnapped Helen's two children, raped her sister Eve, and later murdered Miss Betsy McDonald along with seven others from the town of Cat Creek Junction."

The judge then asked, "Who are the defendants?"

Bear stated loudly, "Tatum Forester, Thomas Pickering and Vance Johnson, your Honor, sir." He then pointed at the three men and said, "These that sit here."

The three prisoners sat in the front row, still in shackles.

"And how do you three plead to these charges?" asked Judge Craig.

The elderly Nathan Forester stood up and asked permission to address the court. He was sitting next to his son, Tatum and said to the judge, "I am Tatum Forester's father and the defense attorney."

"What do you plead?" asked Judge Craig.

"Not guilty by reason of insanity," Nathan Forester replied.

"Explain to me," said the judge.

"Tatum Forester and these other men had no knowledge that the war between the states was over. All that they did was a mere act of war they thought was still in progress."

"Sir," replied Judge Craig. "It is now 1869. The war has been over for four years."

"Even so," Nathan Forester added. "They have been isolated in the wilderness."

Judge Craig was quietly annoyed with Forester's explanation. "That is no excuse for the acts these men have committed. Are there witnesses?"

Emma, Charlie, and Eve stood and raised their hands. They quietly stepped forward from the opposite side of the courtroom from Tatum and his men.

"Miss Eve O'Donnell," introduced the bailiff.

Eve was nervous, scared to tell the tale of rape, but Bear had assured her it was the last time she would be forced to relive it.

Judge Craig leaned toward Eve slightly and asked, "What occurred, Ma'am?"

"On the fifth of September, these men broke into our ranch," Eve began, calming herself by speaking slowly. "They grabbed my niece and nephew here and took them away. The men forced me to have sex with them. This one here," she pointed at Thomas Pickering. "In a very brutal manner he forced me."

Judge Craig spoke to Bear. "Was there another man with these three?"

Bear explained, "Yes sir. There was one more man, but he died in the gun battle when we captured them."

Judge Craig then said, "Hmm. Seems straight forward without going into more detail." Then he said to Bear, "Tell me about the murder of Betsy McDonald."

"Self-defense, sir!" interrupted Nathan Forester loudly.

"That ain't so!" shouted out Charlie.

Judge Craig hit the gavel once and said, "Order in the court! We must have order." Charlie still stood before the judge and Judge Craig asked him directly, "And who are you?"

"I'm Charlie Hardin, Sir." His anger was heard as he spoke out. "I stood right there and watched that man," he pointed at Tatum. "Tatum Forester shot Miss Betsy right between the eyes!" He paused and then added, "And she didn't have no gun!"

Judge Craig looked over the top of his glasses and asked, "Did anyone else witness this."

"I did," said Emma in a very soft voice.

"What is your name, Miss?" Judge Craig asked.

She spoke a little louder. "Emma. Emma Hardin."

"Did any of the other defendants take part in this crime?" the judge asked.

Emma and Charlie both nodded yes. "All of them did," said Charlie.

"Well, that's murder," said the judge. There was a stirring in the back of the courtroom as the few men from Cat Creek Junction whispered agreement to the judge's statement.

The judge continued. "It has been witnessed and corroborated. In this territory murder is an offense punished by hanging. I must pass sentence." He banged down the gavel with finality.

Nathan Forester jumped up from his seat on the front row and said, "I beg the indulgence of the court. Sir, can't you see that this defendant is not in his right mind? Is it not the court's policy to dismiss an insane individual?"

Judge Craig said carefully, looking the elder Forester in the eye, "I see the last act of desperation from his father. The three men are set to hang for kidnapping and murder as soon as a gallows can be built." Again he firmly brought the gavel down.

There was a long moment of silence in the room that seemed it would last forever in the peoples' memory. Then Nathan Forester pulled a hidden pistol from his vest and pointed it at his son Tatum and screamed. "The Confederacy forever!" He squeezed off two shots into Tatum's chest so quickly no one could move. Tatum Forester was dead before he hit the floor.

Nathan Forester said, "Your servant." He bowed slightly, put the barrel of the pistol in his mouth and without hesitation squeezed one more shot off. The bullet went straight through his brain and caused a deluge of blood to spray on several people and he too fell to the floor.

There were gasps and expletives as the people stood stiff with shock. A moan went up from the group. Everyone stood aghast at the hideous finality of Nathan Foresters' act.

Two guards came forward and hustled Emma and Charlie from the courtroom. As the general excitement subsided the bailiffs ushered everyone out of the courtroom. Bear cuffed the other two defendants and took them out the back door to the jail.

Emma was pale and shaken. Charlie was clenching and unclenching his jaw, trying not to cry. He had never seen blood like that. It was a shock to his system to say the least. Trying to resolve it to his own mind he said, "Well, I guess that's that."

"Not quite," said his Aunt Eve standing next to him. "There is still the matter of the attack on me to be settled.   I wonder what the judge will do."

Judge Craig stated a sentence on the guilty men for the crime against Eve. It was an almost empty courtroom. Before long Bear came out of the courtroom telling Eve that the judge had sentenced Thomas Pickering and Vance Johnson to seven years each in the Yuma Territorial Prison. They would be transported as soon as the paperwork was filed which dictated they would be in the Durango jail for a month. It was almost all over.

Emma cried thinking of her friend's fate. Bear took her to visit Mr. Vance in the jail. But Thomas Pickering was despondent and didn't even bother to vow revenge in the future when he'd served his sentence.

Eve sat by herself for a long time until she had a hold on her emotions. Helen was just grateful that Bear had helped them get the children back in one piece. Paiute Bill and Marsilla had much to say to one another in private, while Bear's Horse and Dog were quiet about it all.

The only one not satisfied was Charlie. It would be his thirteenth birthday in a few days, and he was sullen about it. "I feel like the odd man out," he kept telling himself. "And I'm not even a man yet."

XI

Charlie was chopping wood, feeling dissatisfied with the world and angry. It was his birthday. Bear rode up on Horse, followed closely by Dog who was in a gay mood, his tail wagging happily.

"What's up Charlie?" said Bear. "I hear you're thirteen today."

"Yeah," Charlie responded in a flat voice.

"I've got something for you," Bear said as he dismounted Horse. He dug into his saddlebag and pulled out the most beautiful shining pistol and leather holster.

Charlie's eyes almost popped out of his head. "For me?" he exclaimed.

"Yep," answered Bear. "For you."

Charlie took it in his hands in admiration, but he fumbled with it and looked like he could eat it on the spot. He checked the action, then smelled the polished leather of the holster. He was filled with joy. He looked up at Bear with gratefulness.

"Let's try it out," said Bear.

"Alright," said Charlie. His eyes were full of a glow.

"Ok, now," said Bear. "Remember, this is a tool, not a toy. It is made to defend yourself, not to use to intimidate people or to play with. Adjust the holster to yourself and put the cartridges in the cylinder. Let's pick a target and shoot."

Charlie could feel the power of the gun and its heaviness, all new and shiny. He admired the carved brown rosewood handle.

"Now it's gonna kick some. It's a .45," said Bear. "If it seems to be too much, hold it with both hands."

Charlie picked an old bucket about twenty yards away for his target. He pulled back on the hammer and cracked off a shot. It kicked a bit and almost threw him off balance, but he hit his mark without any trouble.

"At least with the cartridges you won't have to worry about powder burn on your knuckles," Bear said with a chuckle. Then in a solemn voice Bear said, "You wear it, think about it, make it your friend – but consider one thing. It will kill whoever you aim it at. And unless you're prepared to do that killing, you don't pull the trigger. Remember all you've seen and experienced and that will guide you."

Charlie's chest filled with the rich air of the Colorado high country. Now he knew. He was thirteen years old and he was a man.